THE LONG HOT TRAIL

After breakfast, Eli and the rangers crossed the North Fork of the Red River near the Texas line. The ground showed signs of where some of the Kiowa-Apaches had escaped. But before the riders had a chance to move any further, Eli spotted a buggy charging toward them.

"Stop!" Jeremiah Turpin shouted. In his wagon sat his wife and the luscious blond beauty, Louise.

"Take her back! She's a vile, evil temptress. She came into our house, bathed, and accepted the clean clothes we offered her. And how does she repay us? She scampered down to the dwellings of the red men and seduced every last one of them!"

Eli left his horse and looked at Louise's tear-stained cheeks. He thought he was doing her a favor when he rescued her from the Indians but now he was unsure.

"He's right, Eli. I can't help myself. Ever since I was a little girl all I wanted was to pleasure men. In fact, all I can think about now is having fun with you."

"Not here, Louise," he cautioned, feeling a growing response of his own.

"I don't care where," she whispered.

"We can work our way across all of Texas," the Scout chuckled. "If you're willing, I'm able...."

THE DYNAMIC NEW *WHITE SQUAW*
by E. J. Hunter

#1: SIOUX WILDFIRE (1205, $2.50)
Rebecca's uncles offered her to the Sioux in exchange for their own lives. But she survives—through five long years in the Oglala camp—and learns the Indians' cunning ways. Now she's ready to get her revenge and make her uncles pay! She's sexy, daring, and dangerous . . . and nothing will stop her!

#2: BOOMTOWN BUST (1286, $2.50)
When she hears that Bitter Creek Tulley has rounded up his hardcases and is headed for Grub Stake, the new mining boomtown, Rebecca is fast on their trail. She has a plan that's hotter than a pistol!

#3: VIRGIN TERRITORY (1314, $2.50)
When Rebecca finds Jake Tulley's cutthroats in the Ozark hills, she finds *herself*—entirely in their hands. Using her body for bait and her revolver for protection, she bucks the bad guys and evens the score!

#4: HOT TEXAS TAIL (1359, $2.50)
Following the outlaws' scent like a hungry mountain cat, Rebecca rides straight into Galveston, and into the eye of a rip-roaring hurricane. But a lot more than trash and trees will get blown when Tulley's cutthroats come head on against the vengeance-seeking huntress WHITE SQUAW!

Available wherever paperbacks are sold, or order direct from the Publisher. Send cover price plus 50¢ per copy for mailing and handling to Zebra Books, 475 Park Avenue South, New York, N.Y. 10016. DO NOT SEND CASH.

#15
THE SCOUT

TEXAS TEASE
BY BUCK GENTRY

ZEBRA BOOKS
KENSINGTON PUBLISHING CORP.

ZEBRA BOOKS

are published by

Kensington Publishing Corp.
475 Park Avenue South
New York, N.Y. 10016

First printing: June, 1984

Printed in the United States of America

To Phillip W. Robinson—top gunhand, long time lawman and good friend.

A hardier breed, [the scouts] I have never known. Up before dawn, they would travel all day on a handful of cornmeal and jerked beef. Their knowledge of the land, the Indians and their pecularities astounded everyone. Courage was their common fare and woodscraft their jealously guarded profession.

—John C. Freemont

One

The thirty-odd men waited silently in the sage, watching the smudge of black smoke that spiraled into the clear, blue, Texas sky. They held on tight to the reins of their horses that stood patiently beside them, making as little a target to spot as possible. From the direction of the oily smear, a figure appeared. He pulled his high-peaked sombrero from his head to reveal starkly red-blond hair, and waved the men in.

"Mount up, boys," the leader called out in a dusty cough of a voice. The tough-looking men remounted and started cautiously toward the smudge.

They wore no uniforms, except for some who affected the discarded gray trousers or hats of the former Confederate States, yet had the look of a disciplined unit as they started down into the burning hamlet of Mulock.

Bodies lay strewn in the street. The sparse wood in the few adobe buildings nonetheless smoldered. Only this remained for the men of the Texas Rangers, Frontier Battalion's Company D, to find in the Panhandle of northern Texas.

The paramilitary lawmen of the Lone Star State fanned out, each one covering the other as they dismounted and started checking the bodies for life and the gutted buildings for survivors. What they found, though, were the scalped and tortured remains of men, women, and children. Nothing stirred. Even the dogs had been slaughtered.

The young man with the red hair ambled his horse over to a woman with an arrow sticking out of her back, slid from his saddle and gently worked the shaft loose from between her shoulder blades. Even though wounded like this, her assailants had still raped her. Her tattered skirt lay over her head, exposing her violated flesh. The redhead ignored the dead woman's nakedness, but walked grim-faced to the leader of the group and handed him the messenger of death.

"Kiowa-Apaches," he spat, anger twisting his words and face.

"Yep," the man with the gravel voice answered as he studied the long, thin shaft of arrow with its telltale markings and fletchings. "'Fraid it is."

"I ain't never knowed Injuns to hit something this big or so early in the year, Cap'n," a ragged-looking Texan spoke from behind.

"Must be a reason, Thacker," Capt. Duke Reagan responded.

"You bet there is," the redhead volunteered hotly, wiping his hands on the yellow striped blue pants he wore. "It's that goddamned Red Owl! He's whipping up trouble and, with those filthy red niggers, it don't take much."

"Now, Tom," Reagan started patiently, not wanting to offend his volunteer scout. Many of the men resented the implied Union sympathies of the touchy young man's blue trousers. Captain Reagan softened his voice to take

8

the sting from his criticism.

"I don't know a single white man who claims to have ever seen this Red Owl."

"What's there to see?" Tom Meyers nearly cried back as he arced his hand over the destruction around them. "Ol' Gen'ral Sheridan was right when he said the only good Injun is a dead Injun."

"Actually," the captain answered patiently as he walked over to the prone, bare body Meyers had taken the arrow from. He bent and pulled the once lovely girl's dress down to hide her exposed, violated body. "He said, 'The only good Indians I ever saw were dead.' And he was talking to Chief Turtle Dove of the Comanches when he said it."

"That don't have nothing to do with what we got here, Cap'n," Thacker pressed into the conversation. "There ain't a single person left alive in this town, even though the place was packed with plenty of able-bodied men to put up a fight."

"I don't see much sign of struggle," Reagan ground out of his throat. "Looks like the raiding party walked in without much anybody giving them a thought." The captain paused a moment to study his men out of the corner of his eye, then added, "Powerful medicine."

"And the Kiowas picked up plenty of grub and ammo to boot," Thacker pointed out. "We got real problems." Though the young ranger talked tough, his cheeks were pink and bright and his angry eyes still had the look of a boy. He put a hand through his dusty black hair and sighed.

Lieutenant Wilderspin walked toward his commander.

"Looks like they headed north, Duke," he told Reagan.

"If we ride after them, they're gonna disappear like they've done for the last two weeks," Meyers protested.

9

"'Cept for a few stragglers, they've all gotten away clean."

"I sort of had a feeling something was cooking out there long time ago," Reagan commented. "This talk of a new Owl prophet like old *Maman-ti* had everyone spooked as far back as last fall." The captain took several steps to the north, studying the horizon and meditatively twirling the bloody arrow between his fingers. "These raids have been too well planned, and the Kiowas have been too well armed to be simply an average raid. I need some help with this." Captain Reagan turned back to his men.

"Thacker," he started. "I want you to get up to Kansas City. I got a wire yesterday saying Holten will be coming in on the *Bonnie Gibson* in a week or so. He's gonna wait for you, so you hurry along, fast as you can, and bring him to me."

"I don't know why you need a scout, cap'n," Meyers countered, a stain of hurt in his words. "I'd work for you 'round the clock if I was a Texas Ranger."

"My company's full up," Reagan explained one more time. "Seventy-five men strong, with brothers and cousins behind those men waiting to take their place. You're good, Tom, you know that. But I can't pay you. You're a volunteer. You can only work for us part-time. And considering how tight things are in my budget, I can't find any money to pay you."

"I'd do anything to get me where I can kill those filthy Injuns," Meyers growled back. "I'd go a hundred miles just to piss on a red squaw."

Thacker interrupted the volunteer scout to speak to his captain.

"I only want to know one thing before I start across Indian territory after this scout you're all so fired hot over. Is this army chief scout, Eli Holten, a Texan?"

Reagan sighed, then smiled patiently. "No, Thacker,

10

he's not a Texan."

"Well then," the Texas Ranger answered, "he ain't worth shit." Thacker whirled and marched toward his horse. Wilderspin and Reagan followed to their own mounts, leaving the volunteer scout standing on the edge of the hamlet.

"Eli Holten," Meyers cursed, then spit into the dust.

Eli Holten, chief scout of the Twelfth U.S. Cavalry, nearly shivered with frustration as he held his breath and watched Amy Peters nod her head demurely and whisper, "I do."

Ezekiel Smith, healthy pink cheeks shining, smiled at Holten.

Holten's breath escaped with a lurch. His feeling of personal loss had only been intensified in being asked by Zeke Smith to be best man.

"Then it is my delightful pleasure," the Most Honorable Judge Lewis B. Thornton intoned, "as Circuit Court Judge of the Dakota Territory, duly and legally appointed and sworn, to pronounce you man and wife. You may kiss the bride."

The new Mrs. Ezekiel Smith leaned toward her husband and laid a lip-lock on the reverend that she usually saved for only her favorite customers, sending the gathered congregation into guffaws and peals of laughter. All except Eli, standing to the groom's side, who felt a serious void in the pit of his stomach.

The people of Eagle Butte started throwing rice on the Reverend and Mrs. Smith as the smiling couple dashed toward the front of the newly built church.

"Eli," the judge volunteered to the scout, "that woman will bring joy and children to our dear friend Ezekiel. You should be glad for them. Allow us to repair to the Thunder Saloon to drink to this union spawned in

11

the clouds of heaven . . . and maybe get some color back in your cheeks."

The two men exited the handsome new church and headed for the even more elegantly rebuilt Eagle Butte Thunder saloon. Along the way, men and women waved acknowledgement to the scout, and a gaggle of small boys trailed the pair, shouting Eli's name and cheering. His stock among civilians had never been so high, nor his spirits quite so low.

"Ah, yes, a lovely day for a wedding," Thornton droned as he studied the cloud-spotted cobalt sky and carefully stepped around melting snow drifts and blue, cold puddles in the muddy street.

Holten didn't answer. He could only take note of the hungering ache between his legs that Amy Peters had always nursed away so expertly during the long, cold winter months. He sighed with self-pity at his loss and let his instincts direct him through the bat-wing doors and to the bar. He hitched his leg up and rested a booted foot on the brass rail, leaving the judge to order the beer.

A group of tittering young ladies of the Thunder Saloon came shortly after them, dressed in their Sunday best to send off their former associate and her new husband. They all dabbed at their eyes and spoke in slightly saddened voices, as though at a funeral. Even so, they rushed to the judge.

"Thank you for a lovely wedding, Your Honor," Mimi, the new and undisputed leader of the flock of soiled doves, blubbered. "A more beautiful service couldn't have been done by the reverend hisself."

"You know, ladies," the magistrate started, removing his slightly battered top hat from his balding pate, "there are many ways of expressing one's appreciation to a man, but my favorite is giving him a good deed in return."

Several of the girls giggled in tinkling chorus, hiding their faces behind Oriental ornamental fans, a hot item

12

that a traveling drummer had sold to every girl in the house when he came by shortly before the big snows hit.

"Why don't we take His Honor upstairs, girls?" Suzy, a stunner with long black hair and large firm breasts, suggested with a mischievous smile. "We'll all give him a good turn."

She slipped her arm under Thornton's and led the ladies and the chortling judge up the stairs to her room.

All except Mimi, who stayed behind. She stepped to the bar and rested an elbow on it, then leaned on Holten, who stared morosely into his beer.

"Aw, come on, Eli," she finally blurted, "you should be happy for our friends."

"Did I say anything about not being happy?" the scout countered, his gray eyes snapping fire. "Why, I'm tickled to death, can't you tell?"

Mimi slipped an arm into the rugged man's own and sighed. "Every woman wants to get married, Eli," she explained. "She wants to have children and know who the father is, be taken care of and belong to someone special forever."

"*I* don't want that," Holten spat, although the young, firm prostitute pressed gently against him and warmed his loins with her goodness. "I'm a simple man doing a tough job and loving every minute of it. I could be killed tomorrow and no woman would be left a widow or kids left without a Paw."

"That's why you'll never be short on women who love you, Eli," Mimi cooed, "and that's why all the women you love are gonna run off and marry someone else."

Holten stood there a long time, sipping his beer. He appreciated the silent company of the affectionate girl. His large, sensitive ears picked up the squeaking floorboards and regales of laughter coming from Suzy's room. The sound brought forth another sentimental sigh.

Mimi tugged on Eli's arm.

"C'mon, scout," the chippie challenged. "Let's go up to my room and see how strong my bed is."

"I-I'm really not in the mood," Holten evaded, resisting the urgings of his manhood.

"I'll get you in the mood, Eli," Mimi promised, then snickered. "Besides, when weren't you stiff and ready, all winter long?"

Despite Eli's desire to stew in his own self-pity a little longer, Mimi seduced him up the steps until they slipped into her room.

The soiled dove securely shut the door behind them as she led Holten past the threshold. She executed a graceful pirouette and placed both warm palms on his chest.

"You haven't been to my room since we got out of those damned tents, after the fire," Mimi accused. "What do you think?"

Eli recalled the reason for the fire as he examined his surroundings. Lavender-flocked wallpaper covered the four sides of the room, to waist height, where dark wood wainscoting extended to the floor. A brightly polished brass pitcher and basin rested on a small washstand, fluffy white towels hanging from the spooled rods at each side. A large, plump-mattressed canopy bed occupied most of the space, and Mimi coaxed him in that direction as he considered that perhaps Nate Barlow had done the town a favor without knowing it.

Barlow and his gang of rustlers and cutthroats came into Eagle Butte for revenge against Holten, the town marshal, and the town itself. They burnt the saloon to the ground, along with robbing the bank and the rest of the town and murdering the marshal. Eli had lost another lover at that time, the madam of the Thunder Saloon. She had burned to death in the flames.

Barlow and his brigands paid with a stretch of their

necks, but that didn't bring Allison back. Holten couldn't help but think he seemed to lose his ladies one way or another . . . and entirely far too rapidly. Now Amy Peters, a girl he'd only met before the winter, a lady he'd dream about for years, got married . . . and to a preacher at that! Mimi, however, didn't look like she was going anywhere.

The shapely working girl smiled angel's breath at Holten, spread her legs a bit, reached behind her and undid a few buttons before she spoke.

"Now I promised I'd put you in the mood and I figure to do just that. You sit down and make yourself comfortable while I get ready."

Eli fought a smile as he slid back against the headboard of the professional's elaborate bed and watched as the girl peeled away clothing. The Parisian style dress first, then the high-button boots expertly pulled free. The silky red underskirt slid temptingly off the lady's shapely wide hips.

Small, sheer pantaloons clung tightly over her swollen cleft with its tuft of brown pubic fur. Mimi turned part way from her guest as she worked the tightly bound corset off her torso. It raveled loose and Eli's lungs sucked air to match the breathing space the girl now enjoyed.

"My," Mimi commented over her now bare shoulders. "I do feel better." She turned and undid the fastener behind her back to snap her sheer French bodice loose.

Out flopped two unbridled mammaries, firm and jutting like twin monuments. Eli felt a strong structure of his own building in his trousers. A sigh of appreciation escaped his lips as Mimi chortled while she worked the ruffled pants off her creamy, rounded hips.

"Now see?" Mimi asked. "I told you I'd get you in the mood. From the size of that lump in your pants, I'd say I did a fair job of it."

"You're absolutely right, Mimi," Holten gasped as he set to undoing his britches.

"Here," the coquette offered, swaying to the bed and Eli's side, "let me help."

Between the two feverish sets of hands, the scout's buckskin clothing flew off his frame. His scarred and muscular chest gleamed like old gold in the yellow lamplight.

The last thing Eli needed to worry about at that time was nurturing his self-pity. Amy Smith and Holten's good friend, the Reverend Ezekiel Smith, would just have to get along without it. The throatily murmuring Mimi pressed her breasts to Eli's face, urging the scout to take a nipple into his mouth.

Holten's tongue flicked like a whip across the girl's red, left blossom and then he suckled like a newborn calf before letting the hardened nipple pop out. He worked his way down the girl's chest, belly, finally to the inviting thatch of curly hair that hid the gentle womanly cavern that earned Mimi her keep.

The soiled dove jumped with galvanized excitement when Eli's tongue penetrated her outer portals, then she settled down to the warm flow of moisture that suddenly burst inside her. She cooed like a partridge and let the tension build in her body, to make the release come all that much more pleasurable. Mimi urged Holten on, all the time rocking her hips until she couldn't take it anymore.

With a shudder and a jerk, a *petit mort* shivered through her body. Her breath shallowed with excitement as the fluid in her heated, then simmered in her cooking bowl. Mimi pulled away from the hard-breathing Eli. She fell to his swollen shaft and took him all into her mouth with one hungry gulp. Quite a feat for so small a girl.

Eli struggled up to the top of the bed, then grabbed

the headboard as Mimi threw her whole heart and soul into the ministrations she practiced on the scout's throbbing shaft. Holten marveled as he felt the working girl's mouth and throat muscles ripple up and down his blood-engorged phallus.

"Aw-w-w-h, damn, Mimi," Eli cried. "That's some powerful loving you've got there."

Then, over her guest's protests, Mimi backed the pulsing love-lance slowly out of her mouth and grabbed it in both petite palms. She began to rub the loose skin sideways as she stroked up and down.

"I want you deep inside me," she begged.

"Then get up here before I explode all over the bed," Holten ordered in a voice of love. She crawled to the headboard and the scout worked her under him. His vibrating manhood hesitated a moment over the tempting moist orifice that bubbled like a brewing cauldron for him, then plunged into the liquid container that greeted him with a new pulsing motion that drew the rugged plainsman to the hilt even before he'd settled into stroking.

Mimi cried out. She kept crying for a solid ten minutes.

"I . . . came!" she declared in wonder at the top of her lungs. "I know it ain't ladylike to say that, but I came like all the hills was busting open! Oh, God, how good it feels, Eli."

"Less talk and more action," Eli grunted in high good humor.

Suddenly the door burst open to his left.

In one swoop, without pulling his plunging wick from its warm, cozy reservoir, Holten brought his Remington .44 out of the pile of clothing at the side of the bed, cocked and aimed it at the figure in the doorway.

A young, pink-cheeked trooper stumbled through into the room, brought himself to his full height, blushed

17

bright pink at the sight before him and snapped a smart salute to the brim of his perfectly placed kepi.

"Trooper Homer Pettigrew reporting with a message from General Corrington for chief scout Eli Holten, sir! Are you that person, sir?"

Eli resisted shooting the trooper dead, but couldn't suppress a cry of frustration.

Two

An hour later, Eli sauntered into the office of Gen. Frank Corrington, commander of Fort Rawlins, home of the Twelfth U.S. Cavalry.

Corrington looked up from his large oak desk, smiled when he saw his unannounced visitor. Without a word, he rose and turned to the small covetous liquor cabinet to the side of his desk, placed two snifter glasses on the finely polished rosewood platform that doubled as a miniature bar, hesitated with a glance at the gangly chief scout, then reached to the back of the cabinet to pull a fine crystal decanter which a crimson-hued liquor filled nearly to the top.

Eli froze at the sight of the container. It only came out when a tough assignment was in the offing. Experience had long ago taught him that Corrington gave only the tough jobs to one Eli Holten. Nervously he pulled his gray slouch hat from his head, exposing the curly blond hair. His deeply bronzed, hollowed cheeks lost a bit of color. From the size of the shots the general poured, this meant *big* trouble.

"Getting the good stuff out, huh?" he volunteered.

"The best," Corrington answered. His wide-set, pale blue eyes twinkled, though they avoided gazing directly into those of his chief scout. "Take a seat, won't you, Eli, my boy?"

Like a mountain lion settling into its lair, Holten sat gingerly on the edge of the expensive black leather upholstered chair, prepared at any moment to spring at the first sign of danger. He could smell it in the air. Next thing he knew, Corrington would start to stroke his full, neatly trimmed mustache with one long, spatulate finger. A sure sign that difficulties were on the way. The general smiled and lifted high the generous libations he had dispensed from a supply Holten knew the commanding officer hid from visiting senators and high-ranking officers. He realized his problems worsened with every drop of brandy that had dripped into the cut crystal balloons.

Corrington handed Holten the vessel with slightly more of the potent fluid. Yes, a damned hard one coming up, Eli evaluated.

"Cognac," the general boomed in forced affability.

"Yes, sir," Eli answered evenly, with considerable reserve.

"Fine Napoleon brandy," Corrington pressed.

"Yes, sir," the scout dutifully repeated.

"Care for a cigar, Eli, old friend?"

"Sir, couldn't you just tell me what it's all about so's I can step out back and put a bullet in my head?"

The commander of Fort Rawlins chuckled good-naturedly and ignored the fact Holten might well be half serious as he slid two long Havanas from a carefully kept humidor box at the front of his desk. The general clipped the twisted end of one and inserted it into Holten's mouth, then began to speak as he lit a lucifer and set it to

20

the rolled tobacco.

"I'm going to start by telling you a story, Eli," Corrington began. "Back toward the end of the war, in fact, a lot closer than anyone imagined, I was out inspecting the troops toward the front of our positions. We hadn't fired an unfriendly shot in about a week, things had grown pretty peaceful." Corrington clipped his own cigar, moistened the end in his brandy, then set to lighting it.

"This night, though, I dismounted to . . . ah, relieve my bodily functions . . . and suddenly all this rebel howling is coming up from around me. I was caught literally with my pants down right in the middle of a Confederate attack. My horse spooked, Eli, and, needless to say, I was captured. I figured I was going to take one unpleasant trip to Andersonville or suchlike as those Johnny Rebs marched me to their commander." The general ambled contemplatively back to his overstuffed leather chair behind his desk and sat down before continuing. His face brightened and he looked Eli in the eyes.

"But I was wrong. I met an acquaintance from West Point, old Duke Reagan. He'd been a few years my senior, but we'd ended up in the same unit before hostilities began and before he headed back home for Texas. Why, we hit it right off." Corrington adjusted himself in his seat. "You know how it is, the gallant Southern officer and me, the urbane professional soldier. We found my situation to be the height of good humor."

"How bad is this going to be?" Holten asked around his cigar.

"Don't interrupt me while I'm reminiscing," General Corrington rebuked softly, then continued. "Before the next day, before the colonel could ship me off to some prison camp, word came the war had ended nearly two weeks ago, with Lee signing his surrender at Appomattox." Corrington paused to steal a sip from his cognac. "Well, ever since then, we've kept in touch. Colonel Reagan of the Confederate States' Army is now *Captain* Reagan of the Texas Rangers, Company D of the Frontier Battalion, stationed at Lubbock in the Panhandle."

The Texas Rangers! Eli felt a flush of adrenaline as his never ending urge for adventure fired up. Those boys supposedly found trouble and excitement everywhere they looked. They ran Indians to ground, shot it out with desperados, enforced the laws of Texas and protected the lives and property of the citizens. He recalled the story, much reprinted in frontier newspapers, of the small town in Texas where a food riot had begun. The mayor sent for help from the rangers and, when the train arrived the next day, off stepped one ranger. Astounded, the city fathers demanded to know where the rest of the rangers were. "You have one riot, right?" the ranger asked. When assured that this was indeed the case, he responded, "One riot, one ranger." Tough boys, all right. Abruptly, Holten realized that Corrington had continued talking.

"Apparently, Duke has been smelling something wrong down there ever since last fall. The Kiowa-Apaches have a new medicine man, in the vein of old *Maman-ti*."

Holten straightened up. "But . . . the Comanche and Kiowa owl prophet died," he protested. "He didn't last two months in that Florida prison."

"This man is being called Red Owl," the general continued with a sage nod at Holten. "The raiding season has started way too early, and they're hitting big targets, towns as well as ranches, with incredible accuracy . . . well, it's become obvious there's some powerful medicine involved.

"All of a sudden, the Indians seem to know where the rangers are all the time. Captain Reagan can't catch any

22

of the raiders even to question. He's suspicious about the movements of one particular trader, but he can't catch him dealing with the Kiowa-Apaches, or the Commanches, or being in possession of firearms or whiskey. Captain Reagan needs someone down there who's an expert tracker, a superior gunhand, and someone who knows a damn sight more than he how the Plains Indians think."

"How do I figure into all this?" Holten asked, knowing the answer and wanting to make the general spell it out.

"We-l-l," Corrington hesitated. "I've been bragging on you. For quite some time I've been telling Duke how I've got the finest tracker in this country working for me and the Twelfth. I volunteered you to go down there and straighten everything out."

"Uh . . . just like that?" Eli countered. He thought a moment. He'd wanted to winter in Texas, only Amy Peters and the ladies of the Thunder Saloon had distracted him. Now that Amy was married, he certainly had no reason to stay.

"First of all," Holten started, taking a quick gulp of his cognac, "I know Sioux, not Kiowa-Apache . . . and with a name like that, what are they mostly? Kiowas or Apaches? Second, who could track better than a bunch of Texas Rangers?"

Corrington pointed at Holten. "I have boundless faith in your talents, Eli. As to the tribal antecedents of the Kiowa-Apache, the way I hear it, they began as outcasts from both tribes. Once the Apache ranged as far as Texas and into Colorado. The Kiowa claim to have come from up in the Yellowstone country. As they moved south, they must have rubbed shoulders with the Apache. Something besides sparks must have flown. Out of those encounters came the band that is now known as the Kiowa-Apache. Few of 'em, but meaner than the devil with a pitchfork up his ass."

23

The truth be known, things looked mighty bleak in the Dakotas anyway. All the Indians seemed resigned to their fate. The "blessings of civilization" quickly crept up on the formerly wild and wonderful land, bringing such social reform as the Women's Temperance League and ministers preaching against houses of ill-repute, liquor, and cards. Things were getting entirely too calm. Texas looked like a much more inviting place than the high plains right about now. Eli pondered this and shrugged.

"All right, I'll take the job. What are they paying?"

Corrington's face twisted in several unique directions as he fumbled and squeezed unrecognizable words out of his throat in response to the question.

"Well . . . ah, ya see . . ."

"You mean they're *not* paying?"

"I didn't say that!"

"Then what's the contract paying?"

The general settled a bit and looked away. "They're, ah, not paying."

Holten started to rise. "Thanks for the cigar and drink, General."

"Holten, wait!" Corrington pleaded in a voice as near to panic as Holten had ever heard.

The scout tapped his chest with the butt of the Havana. "I'm not a charity, Frank. I have to make a living."

"This is an old and dear friend, Eli," Corrington began. "He'd pay you, only he's not getting much funds from Austin. The governor there questions the continued need for the rangers."

"What do I do for food and the like?"

"Well, I was going to give you a little something," Corrington said through a sigh. He leaned forward onto his desk, elbows bracketing a square of buff blotter, chin cupped in his hands. "What I sorta had in mind was . . . to leave you on the books here, instead of giving you a leave of absence."

Eli stood still for a moment, absently flicking ash on the floor, letting the general's words soak in. He returned to the black leather chair and sat again.

"You know, General, that's fraud," Holten pointed out. "You're so damned honest, I've been embarrassed for you on more than one occasion. I can't imagine how you got so far, being so . . . so decent."

"Duke Reagan is an old and dear friend, Eli," Corrington answered. "He treated me like an officer and a gentleman that evening when the South and its dreams were fading with the day. I respected that and will always hold Duke in my warmest of memories. A slight, ah, dereliction of this sort is . . . is understandable under the circumstances, don't you think?"

"General," Eli announced as he squared his shoulders and finished off his drink, "I'll go."

"Good man."

Holten leaned close to the commanding officer. "But I have no qualms of guilt about you leaving me on the books, so don't hesitate to deposit my money in a safe place."

The men exchanged solemn winks.

Red Owl dreamed on a windswept hill. He had taken no peyote, nor had he fasted. The trancelike state came of its own accord.

A great owl swooped through the hills and bluffs of Palo Dura Canyon in the Panhandle. It ruled the sky, struck terror in the field mice and vermin that scampered away from the shadow of the great bird. It was a dream Red Owl had become accustomed to. A vision that foretold his own importance. Yet, a new feature had been added this time. From the north came a warrior dressed in strange clothing; moccasins of unfamiliar design, hefting a bow and quiver of arrows marked in yellow and green. When he drew closer, Red Owl saw that this Indian warrior's skin shone with silvery whiteness as though in the light of the full moon. A shudder of fear ran through the dreamer. He needed no other medicine man to interpret what he saw. He stood in his trance and cried out to the warrior for his name. In the dream world, no apparition could refuse to answer Red Owl's commands.

"Tall Bear," the warrior answered haughtily in the language of the Dakota.

"What is your white name?" Red Owl demanded.

Without hesitation the white warrior answered.

"Eli Holten."

The scout sent a hasty letter back to Eagle Butte, explaining only that he had an important mission to perform and wouldn't be back for some time, then he set about packing his worldly goods, which didn't take long. His bowie knife hung on his hip and an extra skinning blade went into the saddlebags. A Remington .44 revolver rode snugly in an army issue holster with its flap cut off and a Winchester Model '73 lay encased in the scabbard on Holten's horse. Eli got plenty of ammunition from the armory, which he stuffed into his saddlebags, along with his meager supply of clothing, adjusted the cinch on his saddle and stroked the neck of his most valuable possession.

Sonny, the big Morgan General Corrington had given Holten at a time that seemed eons ago, breathed out appreciatively, then sniffed at the buckskin clothing that hung on the tall, lean frame of his master. The scout adjusted his floppy hat on the top of his head and made sure his animal friend was in good shape. He checked Sonny's hoofs and the knobby swellings around the beast's leg joints, inspected the fit of the saddle and the bridle. Oats and some sugar for Sonny rested in a gunnysack tied to the skirt. Arbuckle's coffee, dry beans, a greasy slab of bacon, cornmeal, and some buffalo jerky occupied another burlap bag, which lay on top of two cast iron skillets, a granite coffee pot, and a small wooden coffee grinder at the bottom of one saddlepouch. Eli ended his examination at the sound of approaching footsteps.

Sfc. Michael Dohoney Morrison, with his pot belly stretching at his waistband and distending his suspenders, stepped up and slipped a quart bottle on top of the load.

"Now don't be far tellin' me ye won't be needin' it," Morrison announced in his rolling brogue. "Sure it's a long way to Pierre and the steamboats. Further still to Texas."

"If you think I'm going to refuse your gift," Eli returned through a laugh at the pink-cheeked, red-nosed sergeant, "you've been drinking too much of your own stuff."

Morrison flashed an impish grin. He raised his big, hairy right paw and solemnly intoned, "Sure an' I've not touched a drop since . . . since . . ."

"Last night?" Eli prompted.

"Ye wrong me, bucko!" the first soldier of C Company declared. "It's been so long, I've plain forgotten."

Eli bent closer and sniffed the nco's breath. "Strong coffee you brew in that orderly room, Sergeant Morrison."

The Irishman's face flushed. "Ah, go on wit' ye. Ah . . . here comes the gen'ral. Ye'll not be, ah, revealin' all ye know, now will ye?"

"Of course not, Michael me boy," Eli assured him in a mock brogue.

General Corrington and most of the men off duty began to gather around as their favorite scout pulled himself into the saddle and waved them all good-bye.

Their shouted well wishes followed him out the gate.

Eli headed south, working his way across the miles of flat plains, the buffalo grass brown and frozen on the desolate ground of early spring. Or worse, cold mud frequently sucked at Sonny's legs as they forded creeks swollen by the melting snow. Occasionally he had to find ways of crossing rivers clogged by ice and uprooted trees and turned into temporary lakes. He hazarded it all without question or complaint and with consumate skill. His heart beat lightly in his broad chest for he was doing what he loved best: following the quest for adventure.

The town of Pierre, Dakota Territory, situated itself on a long, narrow peninsula that jutted into the Missouri River. A small hamlet, it boasted the largest riverboat docks on the Missouri, north of Kansas City. The town slept in somnolent ease when Eli rode in at mid afternoon five days later.

Despite the increasing warmth of early April, the town still looked like a place under siege from the elements. The condition of the streets outdid the plains, treacherous with chuckholes, gray mud sticking to Sonny's surging fetlocks. The townsfolk navigated along planks of wood laid out over the mud streets, while horses shivered as they stood tied outside the drygoods store and the many saloons and bawdy houses.

Eli spotted a small boy playing along one boardwalk and called out to him. "Can you tell me where the ticket agent and telegraph office are?"

The boy looked up with awe at the tall stranger in buckskins, bristling with weapons, before he found his squeaky voice. He pointed one grubby, nail-bitten finger down the road.

"The ticket office for the river packet is right there next to the docks. The telegraph office is just up the street from there, at the stage station."

"Thank you, son." Eli flipped the boy a shiny fifty

cent piece, tipped his hat and started down the road. Right where the youngster said, next to what Pierre called the docks, though they looked like nothing more than tree stumps for the steamers to tie up at, Holten found a sturdy one-story building with a fading sign that announced, *MISSOURI RIVER PACKET . . . TICKETS.* Below the words, a black-painted space, divided by a vertical white line, provided room to post schedules. Shaky scribblings in chalk announced an arrival that afternoon at four and a departure south the next day at eleven o'clock in the morning. He entered through the stout oak door with a beveled glass panel.

Eli paid for a first class ticket, which provided deluxe accommodations aboard the steamboat. Then he went up the street and sent a telegram to Kansas City, Missouri, in care of a hotel where Corrington had been told a ranger would be staying, waiting to escort Holten to the Texas Panhandle. Eli addressed the telegram to Texas Ranger, Company D, and said he would be arriving shortly. His chores accomplished, Eli set out in search of a bed, a bottle, and some female companionship . . . not necessarily in that order.

Three

The Kiowa-Apache warriors gathered in a secret place, close to where Red Owl stayed, and howled hysterically, with the power of the prophet, the mystery of their mission, and the strength of the firewater in their bellies. Leroy Barker, oblivious to the words of the holy man on the stone, handed out crockery jugs of rot-gut to the wildly screaming savages who made him so much money.

"There is a way!" the prophet shouted from a large rock, through the owl-head mask that magnified and made his words sound hollow. Bathed in the glow of a red sunset, his face deep in shadows, he took on an appearance of the supernatural.

"The buffalo are not gone, but are changed deep within their All-Spirit by the presence of the whites. They can be brought back!" More howls from the paint-smeared warriors who shuffled proudly through dance steps around the boulder.

"But the way is not easy and is full of danger," Red Owl warned. "I cannot promise you a simple path. Even I do not understand all that must be done. The owl has told me this. I learn with every day, and I ask you to follow now, for the owl has told me I must search you warriors out. Men with strong hearts and mighty arms for battle."

Again shouts of approval rose. Red Owl hoisted his *coup* stick over his head. From its tip hung a lone white man's scalp, though all the gathered warriors knew that Red Owl had taken many more.

"For every white man you kill, I have been promised the return of one buffalo bull to the Plains."

A murmur went through the warriors. It seemed hard to imagine, difficult to grasp that the murder of the whites could directly deliver a buffalo home to the Staked Plains.

"For every white woman that is sacrificed or tortured," Red Owl continued, "we will find ten cows joining those bulls. This the owl has told me and I do not think that owl can lie like the white man."

The dancing and singing had stopped. This was something the braves had to think about. The red one did not promise booty or women, or adventure and *coups*. Instead, he promised a direct connection between killing white men and more buffalo. Powerful magic indeed.

"What about the children of these whites?" a warrior to the back of the raiding party asked. "Do we not keep them as slaves? Or do the boys count as men, the girls as women? Or must we wait until they grow up to kill them?"

A ripple of laughter went through the assembled braves. Red Owl turned away thoughtfully and studied the sky.

"I have not been counseled yet on all this," he admitted when he again faced his audience. "I know of a Crow brave who once told me that white men are nearly as gods, but so foolish. I thought him stupid at the time. Now I wonder. Perhaps if we raised the white children as members of the People, they might grow up to be real human beings, not foolish pale faces . . . and maybe still near to the gods. I counsel that we take them home with us when we can. If I am told otherwise, I will inform you.''

"How can we be sure you are a prophet and not merely misled by your own hopes?'' another, younger, warrior asked.

Angry mutters rumbled through the long-time followers of Red Owl. Red Owl paused for what seemed a long time. Suddenly the form of a giant white owl flapped down out of the sky and grabbed his shoulder.

No one could have looked more surprised or shocked than Red Owl, who gaped at the mighty creature, oblivious to the blood the owl's clinched talons drew from the prophet's broad shoulder. It screeched with ear-paining noise and shook its beak. From that powerful maw fell the corpse of a tiny white mouse. Almost as suddenly, it lifted from Red Owl's shoulder with a lunge.

A silenced moment slipped through. Then the prophet, crimson fluid dripping freely from his punctured flesh, turned his shadowy face to his slack-jawed questioner.

"Listen carefully to the east in a little while,'' Red Owl boomed with new confidence. "You killed fifteen men at the white man's village today and nearly as many women. Shortly you will know I am not misled.''

Red Owl jumped from the boulder and strode toward Leroy Barker, who stood next to his wagon. A jug of shine hung from the bootleg salesman's limp hand. His eyes protruded from the sockets like they were being squeezed out, staring into the sky where the owl had disappeared.

"How'd you do that?'' Barker inquired in an awe-filled voice.

"Do you have the guns?'' Red Owl demanded, ignoring this hated white's mystification.

It took a moment for the trader to collect himself, yet his business sense eventually persevered. "You got the money?"

From a leather satchel that hung on the Kiowa-Apache's hip, Red Owl produced a wad of mixed and assorted currency. For years, the paper meant nothing to him, yet recently he had acquired an appreciation for what it could obtain.

"We also gathered gold and other objects at the town. Would you wish to discuss those as well?"

"Later," Barker answered. "Right now I feel the need of good whiskey. I got some under the driver's box. Care for some?"

Red Owl slowly shook his head. "I must speak with some of my warriors. You put the guns and ammunition in the others' hands."

"Whatever you say, friend," Barker answered with a flash of gold-capped teeth.

Red Owl strode through the awestruck Indians to the side of War Moon, a young brave who had already counted *coup* many times. The prophet had made him one of his lieutenants.

"You have much power," War Moon gasped. "You have no reason to prove any more after the owl landed on you."

"The owl came to tell me the real sign that will come from the east," Red Owl instructed. "I have a mission for you that is most important."

"Tell me and I will do your bidding."

"You will ride to the path that the white man uses to drive his cattle north. They call it the Chisholm Trail. You will kill as many whites as you can on that trail. Scatter his cattle and steal his horses. Take what men you wish with you. This is what I ask of you."

"I and my brothers will leave with the first light," War Moon answered.

"There is one more thing," Red Owl continued. "It is possible you will come across a white man coming this way. He will have a river stone, like this . . ." The prophet pulled a small, smooth red rock from a pouch in his sash. On one side it had a simple cross marked on it.

"If the white man produces such a stone, you give him a guide that will bring him to me."

In the east, the distant lowing of buffalo broke the newly settled night air. The warriors of the band stirred and several of the braves leapt to their ponies.

"They will find two hundred buffalo there," Red Owl told no one in particular. "Fifteen bulls and one hundred fifty cows."

The side-wheeler, *Bonnie Gibson* plied straight and sure down the Missouri, its gayly painted decks a contrast to the usually drab stern-wheelers sloshing this far up in the wilderness of the mighty river. Sparks flew from the tall stacks and bright lights shone from the portholes of cabins and the main salon.

Inside the salon, Eli Holten studied the hand in front of him, crunched thoughtfully on the overpriced cigar someone had given him, then made his move.

"I'll see your fifty and raise you fifty more," he told the cardsharp.

With his pencil-thin moustache and quick, darting eyes, the well-dressed Southerner resisted the urge to smile, keeping his poker face as Holten slapped down the money to cover the bet he had made. The hushed crowd held its breath as they waited for the professional gambler to respond.

"I'll see your fifty, suh, and call," he drawled out in a deep voice.

Eli slapped his cards down. "Three queens. Beat that!"

A flicker of amusement danced on the thin, tight lips of the cardplayer. "You had me worried there for a moment, Mr. Holten," he rumbled, then laid his own cards on the table.

Four aces stared up from the green felt tablecloth in front of the gambler. "Luck of the draw," he muttered in insincere condolences as he reached to the center of the table.

Holten's Remington cleared his waistband and the table top, coming to within inches of the dark professional's face.

"I was told by your captain that you were an honorable man," the gambler uttered in the silence that filled the stately cabin of the salon deck.

"Strange," Eli answered calmly as, from the shadows of the rich curtains that divided the women's retiring section of the casino from the men's gaming room, stepped the captain and his purser. "He didn't say the same about you."

"Where should I start?" the captain asked.

"No need to search him too closely," Holten responded. "I think you will find a whole damned deck of aces and full houses in both his left and right sleeves, plus at least a few cards in his handkerchief."

"I protest such slander against the good name of a Southern gentleman and former officer of the Confederacy!"

The captain of the *Bonnie Gibson*, a gray-haired gent with a walrus mustache and full, red cheeks, glared cold, pale blue eyes at the Southerner.

"The South Tenneessee Volunteers, I believe. Though you've never mentioned it by name," the captain drawled back in his Georgian accent. "I have recently been informed you deserted your unit when a large sum of money was found missing from the funds sent to the Volunteers by their families for food and medicine. Purser, search him."

Not a whole deck, perhaps, but certainly more cards than any crooked player could hope to slip into his hand without being conspicuous, came from hiding in the tinhorn's clothing. The gambler turned crimson, then flushed darker red as the captain took the cards from the purser and held them up for everyone in the salon to see.

The card shark turned to Eli and his eyes could have spit fire.

"You did this to me," he growled. "You set me up."

"That's right," Holten sang back. He was enjoying himself. He tucked his revolver back in his trousers. "First night I came aboard I spotted something wrong about you and went right to the captain about it."

"He's good, though," a passenger in a black felt hat and somber gray suit commented. "I never saw him even look hinkey."

"And to think I let you sit with my friends in the pilot house," the captain added.

From seemingly nowhere a small .41 Remington derringer suddenly appeared in the gambler's hand. An icy ghost of a smile danced across his face as he lined the weapon up on the scout's chest. No one had a chance to scream out or think before the dainty handful of death spit hot lead and white smoke.

Only Holten moved quickly enough. A fast twist to the right ruined the gambler's aim and hid the intended victim's actions for a moment as Eli pulled his bowie knife from the scabbard at the small of his back.

The smoke of the derringer chased the bullet past the scout's chest, missing him by inches. Calmly and quickly the gambler re-cocked his weapon as men yelled and chairs crashed over. Then, abruptly, he froze, his poker face paralyzed.

Sticking out of his solar plexus, buried to its hilt, Eli's bowie knife quivered, moving slightly with each painful attempt by the gambler to draw a breath. The derringer slipped from the card player's grasp and struck the floor noisily in the silence. Holten reached out and roughly

37

pulled his knife free. Blood gushed after the blade and the crooked gambler's face went white.

With a careful and deliberate, loose-limbed flow, the gambler sank to his knees, then fell forward under the table.

"I believe these are your winnings, sir," the captain commented with a casual gesture to the mound of bills and coins on the table. The purser inspected the dead cheat. "Many thanks for your assistance."

Eli's eyes doubled their size as he smiled over the booty on the table, then seemed distracted as he remembered something.

Holten stepped over the still warm corpse and wiped the blood and gore off his knife onto the gambler's jacket. Then he took the dead man's satchel, into which he loaded the money. It looked like he'd get paid handsomely for this assignment after all.

"Kansas City in sight," a black steward sang out as he walked through the dining room and salon at noon the next day. "Docking in Kansas City, Mo-Zuri shortly."

The *Bonnie Gibson* moved effortlessly against the shallow waters of Kansas City "dockside." Only a single large dock served the waterfront. The pilot nudged his giant sidewheeler charge up against soft ground. Deckhands jumped from the low bow of the riverboat and hauled lines out to tree stumps at the water's edge. Gangplanks followed shortly and the passengers began to disembark, before the wagons and freight crews could arrive to start unloading the ship's cargo.

Eli gingerly led surefooted Sonny down the simple span of wood that the crew optimistically called a gangplank onto the hard mud of the Missouri shore. His hands held all his goods, except for his saddle and its attachments which he had quickly thrown on Sonny to

38

get him and it all down off the deck of the steamer.

On the river bank a cowboy dismounted from his spotted pony and led the animal toward the disembarking passengers. He walked straight and cold toward Eli Holten.

The scout's sharp eye quickly took note of the approaching stranger. The holster on his hip didn't look like discarded military equipment, neither did it appear like something the cowpoke made himself. It showed the soft glow that came from the polish of much use. A row of cartridges along the belt settled it for Holten. The man approaching him had reason to use his gun often and have it quickly and easily reloadable. So much so that he'd had a holster and gun belt made by a leathersmith. Though young, the cowboy carried himself like a man of authority, as though he would draw his weapon on anyone without much thought. Holten could read that in his eyes. Clean shaven and hair trimmed, the stranger wore pointed-toe boots, with his clean Levi Straus blue denim jeans tucked inside the flared tops. His white sombrero-style hat looked as new and clean as the Winchester the man carried.

He also didn't look too happy. Or friendly.

The cowboy came nose to nose with the scout.

"You Eli Holten, chief scout of the Twelfth damn Yankee cavalry?" he demanded.

"Who wants to know?" Holten countered coolly.

The cowboy tightened his jaw hard enough to crack walnuts. "Me." He thrust a telegram at Holten. "That's who."

Eli studied the sheet of yellow pulp paper. It was the message he had sent from Pierre. The scout looked suspiciously back at the stranger.

"You a ranger? Out of uniform, ain't ya?"

"You ignorant 'er something?" the Texas lawman fumed. "Texas Rangers don't have uniforms. The only

39

things the state supplies us with is food and this here Winchester. Everything else we rustle up for ourselves."

Holten vaguely remembered someone once mentioning something like that about the rangers. Still, Eli warily continued.

"You got any way of proving you're a ranger?"

The cowboy pulled a silver object from the breast pocket of his flannel shirt. A star-shaped badge carved from a silver ten peso coin shone in Holten's eyes. The ranger than handed Eli a letter.

Dear Mister Holten,

I hope you can read. This here is "Wild Man" Les Thacker. He is a ranger under my command, Company D, Texas Ranger Frontier Battalion. He'll guide you here so's you can help us with our problem. He'll also fill you in on what's going on in the Panhandle. I hope you have a safe trip to the magnificent state of Texas.

Very Truly Yours,
Captain Duke Reagan,
Company D, Texas Rangers,
Frontier Battalion.

Holten struggled to shift his Winchester and bedroll so he could refold the letter. He glanced up at Thacker with a fleeting grin.

"I guess you are what you say you are, Thacker," Holten told the ranger. "Sorry for being so careful. I just wanted to make sure you were who you claimed to be."

"Yeah?" Thacker growled menacingly. He pointed with his left hand. "Now it's my turn."

With that, the Texan threw a blinding punch with his right, smacking Eli firmly in the jaw.

Four

Holten's hands clung to the gear that filled them, while Thacker mercilessly pressed his attack. Throwing combinations and solid heavy blows, the Texas Ranger reeled the scout back. At the edge of the water, with one boot sinking into the mud, Eli swung the saddle bags at his assailant, then chucked the bedroll after it. Thacker leaped back onto harder footing and practically growled as he undid his holster and threw it to dry ground.

"What the hell is going on?" Holten shouted.

"Captain Reagan is expecting some high-falutin' scout that has the eyes of an eagle and the brains of a fox," the lean Texan yelled back. "If you're everything that Yankee general of yours claims you are, I figure you can take a stupid young buck like me apart. If you ain't," Thacker warned as he shook a fist at the scout, "I'm gonna break every bone in your face and throw you back on that boat yonder so you'll never sully the sacred soil of Texas with your presence."

"Boy," Eli growled back as his anger mounted in his

41

raging eyes, "you talk real pretty. Let's see if you can make speeches with your teeth missing."

Quickly Eli undid his own gun belt and threw it to where Thacker had chucked his. Holten noticed Captain Pierce of the *Bonnie Gibson* stepped over to the weapons, smoothing his white walrus mustache as he studied the gathering crowd.

The lanky ranger took full advantage of Eli's moment of distraction to launch himself at his intended victim. A dozen lusty voices raised in a cheer.

Like an Idaho rain storm the younger, wiry man punched and kicked into the scout, all hard, stinging fists and pointy sharp boots. Three small boys yelled shrill encouragement. Despite the fury of his attack, Thacker's blows found their mark.

Eli marveled at the tenacity of youth before falling to one knee to slip a fusillade of punches from the Texan and to snap a hard right that caught Thacker squarely in the balls.

"Fight fair!" the waterfront boys piped, clutching their own scrotums in sympathetic agony.

Air whooshed out of the ranger as he stumbled up the river bank, his bleats several octaves above what they had been before. Eli charged like a crazed bull buffalo, ducked some feeble blocking swings to smack into Thacker's already air-hungry lungs and wrestle him up the rise. Legs churning, bodies pressed together, held by powerful arms, they crested the bank and suddenly, to the east, there sprang Kansas City, Missouri.

The prairie queen city bustled along the shoreline as though the ground it stood on had coughed it up. People, ladies in spring bonnets and men in long frock coats and tall top hats, could only pause a moment to study the wrestling country folk as they rushed about in their sense of great purpose. Several women sniffed indignantly, though their gaze never left the combatants.

Captain Pierce followed the two fighters, leading both men's horses, carrying their weapons and Eli's gear. His eyes sparkled and a hint of a smile creased his seamed cheeks. He hummed scraps of a popular tune under his breath.

The fighting men staggered out of the dusty fields onto a muddy street, made slimy by the urine of many draft animals. They exchanged a flurry of blows and reeled onto the boardwalk in front of a general mercantile. Eli delivered three solid punches into Thacker's chest, then snapped a roundhouse against the Texan's jaw.

Thacker's eyes rolled up and he took two quick steps backward, grabbed at the nearest object he could find and slammed an empty kerosene lantern against the side of Holten's head. The metal lamp tore a clump of hair and flesh out of the scout's scalp, over his left ear. Out gushed blood that drenched Eli's neck and the shoulder of his buckskin shirt. The scout backhanded Thacker into the store's porch post, then ground a fist into the Texan's solar plexus as the ranger hung against the unyielding structure.

The captain of the *Bonnie Gibson* sighed and looped the horses' reins over the nearest tie rail. He pulled his pipe from his vest pocket and set to filling and lighting it.

The combatants grappled and stumbled up the street, deeper into town. Several constables approached, nightsticks at the ready, a gleam in their eyes. Captain Pierce stepped forward and waved them off.

"A friendly contest between gentlemen," Captain Pierce explained to the skeptical peace officers. "I can assure you I'm keeping a careful account of damages."

Eli hoisted a hundred pound bag of flour from in front of a grist mill and held it over his head. Instantly, Thacker dove under it to crash into Holten's unprotected chest. The sack slid easily off his back and exploded against the sidewalk planks behind him. The furious miller howled in protest at the mistreatment of his product. The fight seemed to drag on endlessly.

Both men remained thunderstorms of energy as they blackened each other's eyes and pommeled bellies black and blue. The shouts of the spectators drove them to greater exertions. Finally, in front of the Piedemont Social Club saloon, the fight came down to a toe-to-toe slugging match.

Thacker wound up and delivered a hard fist to Holten's stomach. Eli returned the same. The Texan threw a right cross to the scout's jaw. Holten's head snapped back and he shook his face, throwing droplets of blood among the watchers. He stuck to the ranger's belly. By this time, neither man had the strength to block the other's blows. At last, Thacker stumbled back from one sizzling strike to his solar plexus.

Smelling victory, Holten bore in, somehow finding the strength. He peppered the younger man with a staccato of punches to Thacker's abdomen and chest, then threw his whole body into a cracking blow to the side of the upstart's head.

The Texan fell straight back like a sack of coal. His high boot heels thumped loudly on the plankwalk.

For a second it appeared like Holten might join Thacker there on the dusty boardwalk of Kansas City. He staggered two steps toward the prone man, took one back, then two more forward. He bent over, feeling every punch Thacker had landed, and hauled the ranger to his feet. The scout half dragged, half carried Thacker to a watering trough out in front of the Piedemont Social Club. Holten let his opponent fall to his knees, then gave him a light push that guided Thacker's head into the water.

For a long second it didn't look like the ranger would come out of the trough under his own strength. Suddenly, with a start, he burst from the sobering water, sputtering and gasping for air. Eli grabbed him by the collar and a belt loop and led him into the saloon.

The patrons had crowded to the swank establishment's windows to watch the progress of the fight. Now they parted for the victor as he pushed the dripping loser to the bar. Words of congratulations rose from the well-dressed customers and a few applauded.

Thacker landed solidly against the highly polished mahogany counter and absently slipped a foot up on the gleaming gold of the brass rail. Once satisfied that Thacker would not crumple to the floor, Eli let go and stepped up next to him. He signaled to the barman.

"Two whiskeys here, pard," Eli slurred through lips that swelled larger with every passing moment.

"You're gonna love Texas," Thacker announced, spraying blood from his mouth all over the polished bar top as a large shotglass of bourbon slid up in front of him. "Greatest damn state in the Confedracy an' 'course that means the whole world."

Amos Stuckel, wagon master for the sod-busters headed north toward Kansas, across the Indian territory, marveled at just how crazy this trip had become. First of all, he'd never been so exhausted in his life. Never. Second, he'd never gotten that way more pleasantly. It now stood, unfortunately, that between the fatigue of the men and the mounting anger of the women, he didn't think the train would make it to Kansas. The pleasure monster would strike again and again until there wouldn't be an able-bodied soul among men or boys over ten, nor strength enough left in them to fight off the assaults they could expect from their outraged women-folk.

"You gotta do something about this, Mr. Stuckel," one of the wives warned him with the look of a killer in her

45

eyes. "Or else, *we* will. And I can tell you right now, *it won't be pretty.*"

Stuckel could have kicked himself. He should have known something wasn't right when these dispossessed farmers wanted to go to better land they thought lay in western Kansas. The big ranchers had run them out of Texas, now they wanted to trade it for a damned desert. He couldn't imagine anyone wanting to go from Texas to *Kansas*—of all places—anyway. He'd never heard of such a thing. Nonetheless, he'd taken the job and now lived to regret it. If word of what had gone on ever got out, he'd be ruined as a wagon master. That seemed only the least of his worries.

Soon enough, the wagon train would fall into chaos and they would die in the wilderness of the Indian territory. Somehow, he thought with growing dread, only one, the insatiable one, would survive.

A minor problem faced him now. Indians. Kiowa-Apache from the look of them, sat their ponies only a few dozen yards away, weapons ready in their hands. What the hell were they doing this far north? The puzzle troubled him only marginally. Being massacred could only take him from the pain he persistently suffered.

War Moon stared stoically down at the white man's rolling wood. He'd never seen them headed in this direction before. His warriors gawked at the fine things these whites had. Many horses, much of the stinking meat called cattle, and many women. War Moon, however, counted only guns. He had fifteen men with him. They could not hope to fare well against the settlers, who looked prepared to meet them.

Still, War Moon thought, perhaps he could get something out of the wagon train by sheer bravery.

"What they want, Stuckel?" a nervous and extremely tired man asked from his seat at the reins of his Conestoga.

46

"Probably our scalps," the wagon master answered. "But at the moment, they're signaling they want to parlay."

Stuckel could see the obvious leader of the group motion with his lance. Several of the mounted riders with the wagon train fell in behind Stuckel and they proceeded toward the group of redskins.

War Moon and three of his best men approached the whites.

Stuckel raised his hand in the sign-talk for peace. Coldly, War Moon offered it back.

"We come in peace," Stuckel started. "We aren't settling here. We're crossing into Kansas as quick as we can."

"Cof-fee," War Moon answered in passable English. "We want coffee and sugar."

For a moment the wagon master weighed the pros and cons of giving up any of their supplies to the savages. In truth, being wiped out by a bunch of Indians might be a welcome relief from the horror already in their midst. Then a glorious spark of genius came to Stuckel and its light warmed his soul and gave him hope. Stuckel smiled at War Moon.

"Listen, chief. We're all heap big friends of the Kiowas. You're all great warriors and we'd be glad to give you all the sugar and coffee and anything else we can get you. You stay right here, we'll be back."

The entourage of white men rode back to the train. War Moon and his braves looked impassively on, noting the hurried activity generated by their continued presence.

"Get three or four pounds of sugar, all the coffee you can spare, and flour; maybe they'd like flour," Stuckel commanded.

"There ain't that many of them, Amos," an older gent protested through white whiskers. "We can take 'em if

47

they're stupid enough to jump us."

"Someone go get Louise," Stuckel ordered, then explained his plan to the gathered farmers. At first his suggestion met with solid opposition. Several persons used the word, "barbaric." Earnestly, Stuckel pressed his point. The objections to so drastic an action decreased. He waxed eloquent.

Some of the women saw the light and praised the wagon master as a cross between General Sherman and a reverend full of the Word. Others nodded approval, though they remained silent. Only a few men expressed reservations.

A middle-aged woman with a pinched, ungenerous face and leathery brown skin dragged the horror that threatened their safety toward the wagon master. Despite himself, Stuckel took a step back, apprehension clutching his heart for a moment, as little Louise Van Pelton pushed her bonnet back to reveal eyes so blue that one could drown in them. Worry and confusion also showed in her face.

"What are you going to do with me, Mr. Stuckel?" she whispered through pouting, ruby-red lips, a slight loss of color robbing her of her usually pretty pink cheeks.

Stuckel didn't answer. He fortified his courage by looking around at the women. The sour-faced one triumphantly thrust the girl toward him.

"The savages!" she growled. "That's a better place for an animal like this."

"Shut up, Mrs. Bonneberry," Stuckel shot back and he marveled at the sharpness of his tongue. "Or I'll hand you over, too."

Mrs. Bonneberry blanched and kept her peace. The look on the wagon master's face told her this was a matter of survival and not to be made light of.

The sugar, coffee, and flour were loaded into sacks, tied shut, two together so they balanced on both sides of a

48

horse. One of the men bound Louise's unprotesting hands together, then jockeyed her up onto the bare back of the nag with the supplies. Stuckel led the laden animal back out to War Moon. Three men followed him.

The Kiowa-Apaches' surprise could not be hidden. What they saw outweighed anything they could have imagined.

The white men led a horse with a vision of beautiful blond hair and alabaster flesh on its back. The girl looked in her early teens. Her form stretched at her clothes in a thoroughly adult manner, though, and War Moon felt a twinge in his breechcloth as he imagined what the girl's naked body might feel like pinned and writhing under him. His second thought came out as suspicion.

"What you hide from us?" he accused.

"N-nothing, chief. Not a thing," Amos replied. "Chief, we got sugar and flour and good coffee right here." He glanced at Louise's confusion-filled eyes, then pressed on as quickly as he could. "Plus we brought this squaw to tend to you. I noticed you have no women with you, so I thought you might need someone to prepare the coffee and, ah, the like."

War Moon's eyes rounded and a leering, awestruck smile dug at his stoic lips. He grunted in acknowledgement.

"We, ah, have to press on, real quick here, so you go ahead and keep her, all rightie with you?" Stuckel studied the Indians' faces, looking for any wisdom that might make them refuse to take Louise.

War Moon now had an ache in his groin and he grabbed the reins of Louise's horse from the wagon master without hesitation.

"You are good white men," he announced. "No kill." Then he turned his own pony and with a yell of victory, took off.

Stuckel's sense of guilt peaked when War Moon seized

49

the reins. For a moment he deeply regretted his action. She was, after all, white. He knew that chances were, after they'd raped her, they'd kill Louise. He caught Louise's eyes one last time, however, and a ripple of icy dread replaced his remorse.

He'd seen that soulful gaze once before, shortly after meeting her. She'd been taken in by a family on the train the day before they moved out. She claimed to have no home and no family she knew of. She quickly sized up the masculine population of the caravan and a peculiar glow came to her eyes. It was a look of trust, of helplessness, but also anticipation and, maybe, adventure. That cool regard which seemed so innocent and inviting now could be read as a clear warning.

Louise's expression told Stuckel he'd done the right thing. Even now she had started into one of her incursions that had nearly brought the wagon train to ruin.

"Hello, boys," he seemed to hear her say to the Indians. "Do you like havin' a little fun?"

Amos Stuckel breathed a sigh of relief . . . and pitied the poor Kiowas.

Five

Smoke from the tall, fat, diamond stack of the Baldwin, American-type, four-four-zero steam locomotive gritted the air and station depot as Eli and Les Thacker loaded their horses aboard the stock car for the ride to Wichita, Kansas. Above the giant pair of iron wheels on each side, the name, *General McPherson*, appeared.

"Ever been on a train?" Thacker asked.

"On occasion," Holten answered. Les looked disappointed.

"First time for me, comin' here," he explained.

Holten realized the young ranger had been quite proud of his daring new experience. Twenty miles an hour was a breathtaking speed, he realized, to a man accustomed to horseback or his own two feet. Les gave the scout one of two tickets he had in his vest pocket.

"Let's find a good seat," Thacker suggested, his voice betraying excitement.

Two sets of eyes coldly watched the scout and the ranger get aboard the parlor car toward the rear of the

51

train. The pair in the shadows turned toward each other, and the taller one, in a flat-crowned Cordovan sombrero, nodded to the other.

"We'll have to be mighty blunt if we're gonna do it on the train," he commented around a thin cigar he smoked.

"These hayseeds shouldn't be much trouble for you'n me, Lampbertson," the other man, in a bowler and long, gray linen duster responded.

Ike Lampbertson glanced at his accomplice, a man he knew only as Tom. He'd hired him two days before, once he knew Tom could handle a firearm in a most unique and still unfamiliar way to the West. He now wondered if he'd made a mistake. Tom acted cocky, overconfident. Because of that, Lampbertson intended to let him lead the way. Ike glanced once more at the telegram he'd received from his mysterious employer in the Texas Panhandle, a man who called himself Red Read. Read had gone so far as to give Ike code words to be used in messages. This one listed names and dates.

Ike Lampbertson,
Grand Palace Hotel,
Kansas City, Missouri

Meet Texas Ranger Les Thacker, Twelfth Cavalry chief scout, Eli Holten, at Kansas City. Holten arriving by steamboat from Dakota Territory somewhere around the tenth. Discuss weapons with them.

Read

"Meet" meant to identify, "discuss" meant kill. An advance had been wired to a bank account Ike had at the Kansas City Commercial and Drovers' Bank, sent in from Lubbock. Lampbertson put the telegram away and felt the small red stone his employer had given him when they first made their business arrangement and that he now kept in his pants' pocket. Hanging low on his leg, outside the pocket that contained that rock, Lampbertson felt his stiffened bullhide holster with a sawed-short, four-inch barrel Colt .36 Navy. A good shooting revolver, Lampbertson thought. Perfect for what he intended it for. He reached down to pick up his carpetbag and led Tom toward the car that Holten and Thacker had boarded.

War Moon and his men rode a good distance from the wagon train before stopping. The war chief's love staff ached for action. First, though, their position had to be secure.

A gully, with high sides and tall brush to hide the ponies in, gave them the cover War Moon wanted. The Kiowa-Apaches rode their mounts in.

The other braves had forgotten all about the sugar and coffee. What they wanted rode the bareback horse the white man had given them. Their booty's legs protruded stiffly outward from the barrel-chested animal, as she rode far up on the withers of the dun-colored mount. She swayed with the gait and thrust her forked body against the bony protrusion of shoulder blades. Her eyes had become glassy and the small, pink tip of her tongue protruded from slack lips. Her obvious sexual enjoyment from the steady massage enflamed the red men to powerful lust.

Her expectant grimace and silence disturbed War Moon. The thought set off a warning in his head. It reminded him of a Comanche girl he had known in his boyhood who came, in later years, to favor this form of stimulation over all others. Yet, his blood-engorged lance spoke louder.

"Have you ever seen such hair?" Cold Wind grunted out, his voice forced and hungry as he stared at where her dress had become hiked up to expose her ample pubic thatch. "We shall call her Little Yellow Bush."

"She is beautiful and young," War Moon answered.

"Not too young for what we have in mind, eh, brother?" Cold Wind jested.

"No. But she is not young enough to be restrained, to live as one of us. When we are done, we will have to kill her."

"Then let us not finish for a long while," Cold Wind gasped in anticipation.

The horses came to a halt behind the brush, and War Moon leaped from his pony to run to his captive's. He began to drag her roughly from the mount. Louise slid unresistingly into his arms, her eyes locked into his. The party's leader tore at her clothing, ripping the left shoulder from her dress. Before he could get any further, the girl stepped back, reached down and, in one neat swoop, pulled her gingham frock off over her head, to expose her flat belly, swollen pubic mound, and a generous set of breasts that looked as hard and white as sunbleached bones.

"My name's Louise Van Pelton," the girl said through a smile. "And I like having fun."

As though to prove her point, she grabbed her luscious mammaries and squeezed them, showing they weren't made of bone, but were firm and supple pleasure toys. She worked her hands out to the cherry-red nipples that pointed like rosy bullets. With fingers and thumbs she teased them, pulling and pinching at the points as they hardened, until she gasped with the intensity of her play.

She spread her legs wide apart as she stood there, the furry blond wool parting to show a flowering cleft. Dewy moisture shone there in droplets. Slowly, she began to undulate her flaring hips.

The warriors had stood frozen, paralyzed with awe as they watched this white girl perform. Now War Moon screamed a war cry and rushed at her.

Louise's lips blazed across his hard flesh, found his mouth and engulfed it. Her tongue parted his teeth and slid into the hot cavern of his mouth. The war leader reached down to tear off his breechcloth and found two hands already there, working frantically. He stared into her open, hungry eyes and together, Louise and War Moon worked his enflamed phallus free. She gasped at the size of it and a flame of desire lighted the cobalt pits of her eyes. With practiced skill, the girl's nimble fingers toyed with the brave's fleshy spear, inspiring a new gush of blood into the vibrating member.

Quickly the two sagged to the ground, Louise guiding War Moon's lance into her dripping passage. She sighed with delight as the rigid staff parted her lacy folds and entered the slickly oiled canal, driving toward her core. Her hands clasped across his back and urged him deeper, matching his strokes with hard tugs of her muscular walls, as her hips surged upward until her weight rested on her shoulders.

"Oh, my!" she gasped. "Oh, my, this is so-o-o go-o-od."

War Moon stroked hard and fast into the white girl, his large sack slapping against the bottom of her rump. Suddenly she felt a peak coming and lurched against him out of control as she cried out, her eyes rolling up.

"Sogoodsogoodsogood! D-d-don't stop!"

To War Moon, it seemed so short a time before he built to his crescendo, his throbbing penis milked by tricky, muscular rings until fiery fluid burst from his flesh arrow. The two entwined bodies leaped as one, each crying out in their own fashion. The warrior slowed his strokes as he worked out his enthusiasm. Not so Louise, who continued to hump against him until he stiffened a second time and began to respond.

"More," she grunted. "More-more-more. Give it all to me!"

Never had he experienced such delight, War Moon

55

thought in delirious joy, as he found himself surging in rhythm with the unsated girl beneath him. They writhed in their passion, and he felt his organ swell to greater size then ever before. Sticky wetness slicked both their bodies, and he could swear that she attempted to swallow him whole, drawing him from head to toe into the churning furnace that tugged at his tingling lance.

Their ride lasted longer this time. War Moon's belly ached and his head swam by the time that the tiny girl uttered a staccato series of pleasurable "Aah-aahs" and they melted into liquid oblivion.

"Please, War Moon," a shivering voice sounded from behind. "Let me now."

Reluctantly, yet feeling drained, War Moon pulled out.

"Oh, yes. Please hurry," Louise begged in English. "I can't stand it."

Cold Wind urgently fell into place. Louise's legs wrapped around her newest suitor as she rained kisses and soft caresses on the sturdy brave. The surging couple rocked to an ancient rhythm, and Louise threw back her head to cry out in ecstasy.

"Oh-oh-oh-oh! This is more fun than my first time when I was eight. I want you all. Every one of you wonderful boys!"

War Moon leered as he let his breath catch up and decided they'd keep Yellow Bush for a little bit longer.

"We'll take the train to Wichita," Thacker explained. "Then we'll follow the Chisholm Trail to the Panhandle, meet up with the captain at our camp at Las Moras Creek, near Menardville."

"I'm kinda anxious to meet this Captain Reagan," Eli said as he threw his saddlebags on the floor at his feet.

"You'll like him fine," Les assured the army scout. "Great man, braver than anyone I've ever met."

"All aboard!" the conductor cried outside. The whistle blew twice and shortly the locomotive started churning with deliberate, deep-throated bursts of steam. The passenger car lurched as the coupling snapped tight. Spare stock cars ahead were brought back down the line to gather more cattle at the stockyards in Wichita. Some more violent jolts followed as the rear cars' and caboose's links also bore the strain and added their weight to the engine that labored to overcome inertia. Determined bursts of black sooty smoke shot from the locmotive's smokestack, chunks of burning wood coals ground to a powder by the toothed gears in the large chamber atop the slender flue. Slipping polished wheels on steel rails squealed, and the chugging of steam-fed cylinders began to build in speed. The Kansas City station rocked away behind them. The train gained momentum. It seemed to Eli that they flew out of the city, across the river and onto the rolling plains of Kansas.

"I love trains, don't you?" a young lady told her male companion, a blond-haired man dressed in a spotless blue uniform of an army lieutenant. She wore a fancy gray serge traveling dress with a matching parasol, a high necked jacket that buttoned down the front. Pointy black shoes completed her ensemble. Fashions, Eli decided, that definitely did not fit on the frontier. A moment after she spoke, she broke into a fit of coughing.

Powdered cinders swirled around the coach, making the ride less than comfortable as some of the smoke and dust slipped into the passenger compartment and stung the occupants' eyes. The girl dabbed a lace-edged handkerchief at her lips and concealed her spasm.

"Think this is bad," Les started. "The trip from Wichita to Kansas City, I rode in the stock car with my horse. The animals didn't seem to mind, but I thought I was going to die. We'll have to clean 'em up before we head out."

Holten tried to picture his beloved Morgan, Sonny,

57

covered with soot and ash. Not a pretty sight. Eli decided to think of something else.

"Why don't you tell me about what's going on down there in the Panhandle, Les?"

Unconsciously the ranger tightened his jaw. "Bad things, Holten. Can't explain most of it.

"It started more than a year ago, when an Injun prophet showed up, talking powerful medicine. They've been jawing in Austin about moving all the Indians in Texas either into New Mexico Territory or north to the 'Nations.' It's all bluster right now, but more than a few people think it's a grand idea. The Kiowa and some of the other tribes already in Indian territory are supposed to be peaceful. But now, the Kiowa-Apaches and others still on the loose figure this prophet, Red Owl, is going to rid the earth of the white men and somehow bring back all the buffalo. I've talked to a couple of friendly Injuns . . . as friendly as Injuns go . . . and they think this Red Owl is some kind of ghost of old *Maman-ti*."

Maman-ti! Eli's eyes froze in a distant stare out the window of the car, lost in the power he knew that name carried. More power to the southern Plains Indians than any white man could imagine.

Satanta, Lone Wolf, *Satank*. All great warriors who had become famous in the Kiowa wars with the U.S. Army. Quannah Parker, Tall Elk, Big Bear, all well known and hated Comanche names. Behind all of them, though, stood *Maman-ti*.

His name meant sky walker, or he-who-touches-the-sky, also called *Do-ha-te*, the medicine man, or the owl prophet. He had been born a Kiowa, but soon his fame and ability outgrew a single tribe.

To the Kiowas he was the greatest power on earth. Their allies, the Comanches, elevated this Kiowa to master over all the medicine men in both tribes. Soon the offshoot Kiowa-Apaches began to accept him. The Cheyenne sang of him for his heroic performance at the

Battle of the Washita, where he rescued many women and children from Custer's attacking troops.

What made *Maman-ti* so feared and respected was his apparent ability to prophesy the outcome of battles, down to describing highlights of the combat, and how many men would be slain. It became the practice to go to him and ask how battles should be fought. He directed strategy and it led to victory after victory, including the Lost Valley Massacre near the Loving Ranch.

The chiefs would gather before the great man and from the dark, an owl would come and land on *Maman-ti*'s wrist, screeching and flapping its wings. *Maman-ti* claimed he spoke the bird's language, and from this oracle he would learn what they should do.

One time the winged messenger told *Maman-ti* that if he took a war band to a certain point on the Butterfield Trail, in Young County, Texas, two parties of whites would pass with only a few hours between them. The first group would be small and easily taken. The war party should not touch them, though, nor should the Indians show themselves to them. The second and much larger party was the one the braves should attack. Some warriors would die, but the plunder and glory would be great.

On May 17 or 18, 1871, General William T. Sherman went with a small escort along the Butterfield Trail, investigating personally the reports of Indian outrages in the area. As the small group traveled between Fort Griffin and Fort Richardson, *Maman-ti*'s band watched. The warriors wanted to attack, itching to count *coup*. It took every ounce of personal persuasion for *Maman-ti* to restrain them.

Three hours later, a wagon train of ten prairie schooners, hauling goods, moved out into open country. *Maman-ti*, with *Satank* and Chief Big Tree, led the more than one hundred braves against the eleven white men.

Only five whites managed to escape. They made a

59

break and hid in thick brush while the Kiowas and their allies brutally mutilated the bodies of the others, slowly roasting the testicles off one man unlucky enough to be taken alive. Sherman rode on thinking the reports he'd received must have been exaggerated.

That ignorance didn't last long, though. Over the next few years the army staged a successful war against the Kiowas and Comanches. On September 27, 1874, Col. Ronald McKenzie surprised and routed the hostiles at Palo Duro Canyon. The troopers killed very few Indians, but captured instead fourteen hundred ponies.

McKenzie had rounded up a large number of horses from the Indians before, only to have them stolen back by the Comanches at night. The colonel ordered all the horses gathered together, then took them to Tule Canyon and slaughtered them. Indians on foot were easier to hunt. The great owl prophet could only urge his Kiowa and Comanche allies to fight on in small groups in a hopelessly lost war.

On February 6, 1875, *Maman-ti* and his friend, Lone Wolf, surrendered to the army at Fort Sill. Chief Kicking Bird, a Kiowa who had worked diligently for peace through all the years, greeted them at the gate and swore he would work for the two great leaders' release. On April 28, *Maman-ti* was loaded into a wagon, shackled hand and foot. He was being shipped to Florida for imprisonment as an incorrigible. *Maman-ti* looked to Kicking Bird nearby and reviled him as a traitor.

On the way to Fort Marion, a medicine man named Eagle Chief told *Maman-ti* he should pray Kicking Bird to death. After some hesitation, the owl prophet agreed. He explained, however, he would die, too. His religion forbade the use of his magic against other Kiowas.

On May 4, *Maman-ti* began to pray. Kicking Bird died suddenly at his lodge. The fort surgeon claimed the peace leader died of food poisoning. The Indians present didn't agree.

On July 28, at the federal camp at Fort Marion in Florida, *Maman-ti* called his friends together and said that he would die three hours after sunup. He visited the other prisoners in the fort that early morning, returned to his bed and pulled the covers over his head. He died right on time.

However, the great medicine man had sons. One especially, named *Tejan*.

". . . so we been snookered all over the Panhandle," the Texan droned on. "They seem to know where we are and where we're gonna be. Sometimes it seems before we even know."

"Any for instances?" Eli inquired.

"This last town. We were riding toward the place when we came across some tracks. Our scout, Tom Meyers, started following them for a while and said it looked like an Indian raiding party. We took off after them, headed along the trail in the wrong direction. We didn't stop until Captain Reagan saw smoke coming from behind us where the town was. Tom went there and checked on it, came back and told us to ride *pronto*, the town had been hit." Thacker leaned back against the firm, cushioned backrest. "It didn't look like a man in the place had gotten off a shot. Women raped. Kids all tore up 'er missin' . . ."

The young ranger bit at his lower lip and stared a moment out the window.

"People deserve better than that."

Eli had sensed someone watching them since the train pulled out. Now he became aware of a man dressed in Eastern clothes, adjusting a holster on his belt, purposely dragging it lower on his hip. The Easterner sat slightly behind him, with another man in a black Mexican rancher's hat. The two obviously were together.

"Where's this Red Owl supposed to be staying?"

Les didn't get a chance to answer. The Easterner in the bowler rose and, with a deliberate theatrical sniff, curled his lip in disgust.

"I smell a Texan," the big man with a slight Irish brogue growled.

"That must be me." Les raised a hand and smiled up at the stranger. "I'm a Texan."

Eli shot a quick glance at his companion. The innocent look in Thacker's eyes told him the ranger took no offense at being identified by his body odor, although the Easterner must have meant it as an insult.

"A Texan, then." The stranger leaned down across Eli and grinned coldly at the younger man. The parlor car grew quiet. Only the chugging of the engine and the rhythmic clack of the wheels cut the sudden tension in the passenger compartment. "I didn't know they let Texans on trains . . . for sanitation reasons, I mean."

Thacker looked like a child who didn't know he wasn't supposed to ditch school.

"Nobody told me," he started. Then the cutting insult came clear in his mind. "Hey, wait a minute! Texans can go anywhere they like. Some that other people ain't got balls enough to go. Who the hell—'scuse me, ma'am—just who do you think you are?"

"I'm the man who's gonna throw you off this train to purify the air," the Easterner snarled. "I hate Texans. Cocky bunch of bastards."

The lady in front blushed. The stranger gave a quick glance at Holten. "And I don't like their friends neither."

"See here, mister . . ." the army officer started.

"Stay outta this, Lieutenant." The ranger laid a hand on the shoulder of the blue-clad man in front of him while his young, sure eyes never left the intruder still leaning over the scout. "Best you let me handle this. And best you take your seat, fellah," Les rebuked the man with a wagging finger. "Or else, I'm gonna have to set you down on that cushion real hard."

"You got two ways of leaving this train, you Texas

scum. You can jump off, or I can throw you off."

Thacker's words came hot and angry, spit like sparks from burning wood catching too fast. "You must be planning to get buried in Kansas, mister. You came a long way for your own funeral."

Sitting below the Easterner, Eli knew this had to be contrived. The man's partner sat silently, even as the scout bided time, watching to see how . . . and better, why, things progressed. Though Thacker saw nothing but red, and maybe a point of honor, his beloved Texas's name had to be defended in this confrontation. Holten waited for the next boot to hit the dirt.

"You gonna shoot me dead, boy?" the stranger challenged.

"I will before you throw me off this train. No prissy fool from back East is gonna throw a Texan off any train."

The man in the bowler hat took one step back. "Then make your move, boy. But, I'll warn you, I'm a fast draw with this iron."

"Huh?" If ever a question had been asked with more hostility, Eli had not been there to hear it.

"I said, I'm a fast draw with a revolver."

"Mister," Les started, coming to one knee on the plush red velvet of the horsehair-padded seat. "I don't know what a fast draw with a revolver is, and I couldn't care less, but any Texan can do anything better than anyone else with a shootin' iron. Especially some sissy from the East stupid enough to insult the glorious Republic of Texas."

"I seem to recall us Easterners kicking ass on gutless cowards from Texas, an' all you other rebels."

Les's anger got the better of him. He shot up from his seat and charged the man with the dandified clothing. The Easterner's motion looked blurred in the fraction of a second it took to draw his weapon, point from the hip

63

and fire his Remington .44 Army.

Three things worked to save the young ranger from instant death. First, the train lurched in that fraction of a moment of draw and fire. Second, the conductor chose that same moment to kick the front entrance open and yell, "Water stop." Third, the young lieutenant instinctively jerked to cover the young lady, attempting to protect her from harm, although the round had been expended long before he reached a point of covering his charge. The movement to the would-be killer's right and the bellowing conductor behind him distracted the shootist for the length of a wink.

Les Thacker whirled with the impact, his shoulder smeared red from the strike. The .44 slug spun the Texan off the seat, over the backrest into the lap of a middle-aged old maid who started screaming before Les's hand could get settled in that unused female flesh, his blood staining her conservative dark blue cotton dress.

The Easterner brought his handgun up as he cocked it and turned his attention to Thacker's companion. A .44 slug caught him solidly in the breastbone. As women found their voices to join the wailing maid in a chorus of screams, the big Easterner lept back. He fired into the floorboards before he collapsed under the powerful blow of the heavy lead death. Blood bubbled to his lips and his eyes rolled up into his head.

A Colt .45 appeared in the lieutenant's hand, too late to help Eli as the scout thumbed back the hammer of his smoking Remington. Eli hadn't waited for a further demonstration of the fast draw from the East. Now he looked for the man's partner.

The seat across from him where the Easterner's sidekick had been was empty. Both the army officer and Eli ducked low into the corridor between the seats, the lieutenant facing forward, Holten looking toward the rear. The two men hunkered back to back.

Six

"What are we after?" the soldier asked in a whisper.

"The man in the black Mexican hat," the scout answered. "He was with that foul-mouthed idiot."

For a second the two men struggled to keep their balance. The engine braked. A quick glance out the window told Eli a water tower and a puny three-shack town rocked toward the slowing train.

"You all right, Thacker?" Eli inquired.

"Hell, yeah," Les answered, his voice groggy. "'Scuse me, ma'am. I'm a Texan. Gotta hit us with a Texas-sized cannonball to kill us."

The young woman with the lieutenant pushed past the two armed men.

"Stay down, Elizabeth!" the officer boomed. The girl ignored him to rush to the screaming old maid.

"Hush, dear!" she scolded in a tone one used on wayward children. She tapped the woman on the shoulder. The spinster stopped screaming, although she cringed as Elizabeth tried to move Les, who tensed and gritted his teeth before he would make a sound. His blood soaked the older woman's dress.

Eli raised his weapon and uncocked it.

"He's gone. Probably bailed off the train and into those shacks."

"We could go after him, mister," the conductor suggested as he crawled off the floor where he'd thrown himself when the shooting started.

"No need," Eli countered, staring out the window. "He'll find me soon enough."

"He's lost a lot of blood," Elizabeth remarked as she prepared to bandage Thacker's shoulder. Color had left the Texan's face seconds after being hit, and now his complexion turned to an ashen gray.

"I'm gonna be all right," the ranger countered. "I've been hit before. Seems I can't get out of a bullet's way. They come at me like bees on a bear in a honey tree."

"Well, this bullet went in and out, missed every bone and ended up right here." Elizabeth tapped on the bloody wall post, where a splintered hole announced the final resting place of the fast draw's lead slug. "I'd call that lucky."

Eli reached down into his saddlebags and pulled out Sergeant Morrison's going-away gift.

"Before you bandage that up too tightly, let me clean it out with a little whiskey."

The Texan let out a whoop of pain as Holten poured a generous portion from the half filled bottle into the wound and on the bandages. The soldier had reholstered his service revolver and introduced himself to Eli.

"I'm Lt. John Taylor of the Sixth Cavalry assigned to Fort Sill. This is my wife, Elizabeth."

Holten touched a hand to his gray slouch hat and nodded at the woman as she looked up from her patient to acknowledge the introduction.

"I'm Eli Holten, chief scout for the Twelfth Cavalry up

at Fort Rawlins, and this here youngster is Les Thacker of the Texas Rangers."

"Chief scout." Taylor's eyebrows raised with surprise. "Long way from Dakota Territory, scout."

"Getting further all the time," Holten agreed.

The train started on its way again, the tracks ahead now aimed more west than south.

"How far are you going?"

"Wichita."

"That's where the missus and I are getting off."

"I think you better take him to a doctor when we get there," Elizabeth suggested in regard to Thacker. "He won't die, but it might be good to have it cleaned proper and get Mr. Thacker some rest."

"We gotta get to Captain Reagan as soon as we can." Thacker tried to rise to his one good shoulder as he spoke. Holten leaned down and pushed him back to the seat he stretched out on.

"A few days won't make much difference. Can't have you dying on me, ranger."

Les's eyes reflected the turn of his mind. "Did ya' see how that guy got that six-gun out? Have you ever seen anything so sudden?"

Eli looked up at the conductor and several volunteers as they dragged the dead gunslinger out. He spoke quietly to Les.

"He would have killed us both if the train hadn't lurched."

"And if his friend hadn't run out on him." Taylor slid into a seat and turned to talk to Eli. "I've heard of this fast draw thing. Sort of a twist on dueling, using revolvers as I understand it. But it's the mark of a professional assassin, certainly not a gentleman." Unconsciously the fingers of Taylor's left hand found the thick gold crest of his West Point ring and began to twist it around the third digit of his right hand.

67

"That's why I think the other one will be back." Eli also took a seat and passed around the bottle. "I believe that boy was paid to kill us, Les, and the other one will probably want to finish the job."

"But they weren't Injuns," the ranger protested after a deep, satisfying swallow of whiskey. "It can't have anything to do with what you're coming down to Texas for. No redskin hires a white killer."

Eli looked out the window at the flat, spring-green prairie they rumbled through. Here and there along the way, square black patches showed where the sod had been turned, attesting to Kansas's growing population of farmers. Inevitably, too, Eli saw with regret nearly as intense as that of a cattleman, the sod-busters brought along their barbed wire. More of that "civilization" he sought to avoid.

"You wouldn't think so," he responded at last.

"It may be none of my business, scout," Taylor began as he accepted the liquor, "but I'd like to know what's going on."

Eli explained with all the detail he could about the situation in the Panhandle, how he'd been volunteered by General Corrington to come down and see if his insight into the heads of the Plains Indians could help. He avoided explaining how he was going to be paid for all this. Taylor's young eyes seemed to tighten with these revelations.

"It's my first assignment west of the Mississippi, Holten. I didn't want my wife to come, but since I'll be at Fort Sill indefinitely, she wanted to be with me. Still, if I'd known there was an Indian war brewing so close . . . by the way how far is Fort Sill from this Panhandle?"

"'Bout eighty miles," Thacker informed him. "Texas is a big place. The Panhandle extends right up beside the Nations. That's what Indian territory is called out here.

From Fort Sill, it's about a hunnerd an' sixty miles to smack-dab in the middle of the Panhandle. The damned hostiles raid into Texas, then scoot back to safety at the agencies around the forts in the Nations. There's no call for you to worry about a thing, though, Lieutenant," Les ended cheerily. "Me'n Holten here are gonna get rid of all those Indians long before you can call it a war."

The Baldwin four-four-zero engine made good time across the vast stretch of Kansas, only stopping for water and wood, until they reached Emporia shortly before dusk. There the animals got cleaned, fed, and watered while hungry passengers piled into a Harvey House. None of the yard hands noticed the dark man in the flat-crowned black sombrero who hid in the stock car. Soot from the engine's smokestack covered him, helping to conceal him in the cross braces of the car's roof.

"The food has much to be desired," Lieutenant Taylor noted with an Easterner's predictable fastidiousness as he chewed on the dark meat steak the pretty waitress had brought him.

"Don't complain too loud," Eli advised. "Before the Harvey Houses, all you could get to eat along these Western lines was stale sandwiches and cold coffee. The few times I've been on trains before, I always got a sour belly. If you asked me to compare, I'd have to say this is pretty good grub. Fred Harvey puts out a respectable spread. There's venison, duck, Canada geese, fresh fish, prairie chickens, and buffalo. That's what we're eatin' now."

Elizabeth looked up, surprise written on her face. "It's delicious, darling," she told her husband. "I never thought those shaggy, ugly creatures could have such a fine flavor."

"Sort of sweet," Taylor responded, still unwilling to

relent on the quality of the meal.

Within half an hour, the *General McPherson* chugged into the darkness. Its monstrous oil-burning headlight, all brass and glass, emitted about as much light as a burning pine knot. The passengers slept restlessly on the plush seats.

As dawn broke, better than a mile from Wichita, Eli could smell the town. Before the passengers in the parlor car could see a single building of the rapidly growing prairie city, they saw the stockyards. Although quite early in the cattle-driving season, the crude, but sturdily built corrals burst with gold on the hoof, driven in from holding pastures and ranches west of the farmlands. Holten thought how bad money could smell.

Two-story buildings along Douglas finally started appearing over the sea of beef, though the stench would not abate. The occupants of the car resigned themselves to the aroma of Wichita as the train came to a creaking halt at the station.

A detachment of horse soldiers in clean blue woolen jackets waited on the platform. They sweated mercilessly as they came to attention beside their horses when Lieutenant Taylor helped his wife down the steps. Holten assisted the white-faced Thacker.

"Guess those boys are here for you, lieutenant," Holten observed.

The Taylors turned back to the two men who had been strangers a day before. The officer offered his hand. "I hope you two get to the Panhandle safely. If you need anything I can be of help with, you'll know where I am."

The Texan and Holten shook the officer's hand.

"Thank you for doctorin' me, ma'am," Les mumbled with embarrassment.

"I hope you'll get better quickly, Mr. Thacker,"

Elizabeth answered.

"Oh, yes, ma'am. You don't have to worry about that. I'm a Texan. Why, a little scratch like this'll take me two, maybe three hours to heal. Won't even leave a scar."

The woman's laughter tinkled over the huffing of the still steaming *General McPherson* as she waved over her shoulder, her husband leading his lady toward the detachment.

"Wonder what she was laughin' about?" Les speculated. "Would've been rude to ask. C'mon, let's get our horses."

The young ranger took one step out of Holten's grasp and started sinking toward the wooden platform. Eli caught him before the Texan could get much further.

"Tell you what I'm gonna do for you, Wild Man," the scout offered as he swung Thacker's good right arm over his shoulder. "I'm gonna get you into the nearest saloon, set you down at a table, buy you a couple of drinks and take care of our horses myself."

"A beer or two!" Les's eyes brightened with the thought. "That's the ticket. Why, a couple of cool brews and I'll be like new."

The Good Times Saloon, on Murdock, one of the main, mud streets, offered a clean, bare wood table and products of all three breweries in Wichita. The scout left the ranger in the care of a saloon girl and went back for their horses.

Once the train had stopped, Lampbertson slipped from between the livestock, bridled and saddled his own mount, and the moment the yard hand opened the sliding door to reveal a cattle chute, the killer led his animal out. He ignored the stares of curiosity from porters and townsfolk at the soot-covered image he presented.

Eli arrived at the stock car long after Lampbertson had

71

ridden out of town. He retrieved Sonny and Thacker's wiry painted horse and gathered up their tack and gear. At the nearest livery stable, Holten left Sonny and Les's spotted mustang to be groomed, stabled, and fed. After the scout provided an extra dollar a day, the hostler agreed to two cans of oats for each critter, morning and evening.

"There a doctor in this end of town?" Eli asked the blacksmith half a block along Murdock.

"What's your ailment?"

"A day-old bullet a friend of mine caught."

"Try Dr. Doyle. Retired from the Union Army as a sawbones after the war. Knows everything about bullet wounds. Go up to Broadway and turn right, to the dry goods store, turn left in the alley and up the back stairs and there he is."

Holten returned to where he left Thacker and found the young buck surrounded by saloon girls crowding around, mesmerized by the young Texan's voice.

". . . me'n my partner, why, we're just sittin' there. Eli, that's my partner, he lays back while I lead the fight, see?"

All of the soiled doves nodded their heads, big-eyed as Thacker continued.

"I told the leader of this bunch of coyotes, must've been six'r seven, I said, 'I don't know what a fast draw is and I don't care, just don't take the glorious name o' Texas' . . . *like lightning* . . ." All the girls leaped back with a gasp. "The head honcho pulled his gun and from his hip . . . *from his hip, mind you*, he shot me! I swung around . . ." Wild Man twisted in his chair and leaned into Eli. He looked up.

"Well, hey there, partner. I was just telling these fine . . . er, girls, about how you'n me took out all those bad guys."

"I found a doctor who'll check that wound." Holten's

voice growled as flat as the plains. "I don't want you dying on me from infection before you get me to Captain Reagan."

"First you gotta finish the story," one lovely pink-cheeked lady cried, eyes round with disappointment. The other soiled doves chimed in with agreements. Eli's mind got distracted for a moment. He thought he recognized some of the ladies.

"Now, now, girls," a female voice interrupted from the second-floor bannister above the bar. "He's already told you the story three times. Besides, you wouldn't want to keep chief scout Eli Holten from his duty."

Les leaned toward the pink-cheeked girl. "Eli's a little sensitive about the part where I save him from the fast draw artist with a bullet in my shoulder."

Holten caught none of this. His eyes stayed focused on the madam gliding slowly down the steps toward him. A smile pulled at his lips and he had a flash of fond memories. He stepped to the bottom of the stairs to greet her.

"Della Caldwell," he breathed.

"Eli Holten," Della answered. "I do believe I'm feeling faint with seeing you again."

"I would've thought you'd've forgotten me by now," the scout said as he took the woman's offered hand and did the proper thing, pretending to aid her to a chair.

"In my business, Mr. Holten, it's easy to forget a man's face and name." Della Caldwell smiled demurely. "But I doubt there's a woman you've ever known who can't recall every hair on your . . . chest."

Now they both laughed.

Eli had taken a break from the army some two years ago to lead a wagon train along the Santa Fe Trail and into Arizona. Only instead of farmers and the usual type settlers, he discovered his employer to be Della Caldwell, madam of the best sporting house in St. Louis, the Bird

Cage, which she had decided to dismantle and move to the gold fields of the Mogollon Rim in Arizona, lock, stock, bedboards, and soiled doves.

"What happened to the gold fields?" Eli inquired as he took the seat next to her. Della rolled her eyes and sighed.

"That was some disaster. By the time I started showing a profit, the gold petered out."

"So you brought your folks here," Eli finished.

"Not so many as I'd liked. Wang Che Loo is in the kitchen, trying to make this greasy spoon into Delmonico's. Caesar's still my bouncer. Brian and Mike are still my barmen."

"Is Art Bowman with you on the piano?"

"And still carrying that LeFever Drilling gun of his."

"Then who did you lose?"

Della leaned toward the scout and gritted into his eyes as she counted out. "Candy, Yevette, Michelle, Joyette, Melody, Cindy, Francie, Flora, Angelique, Clarissa . . ."

"Not Clarissa!" Eli shouted protest.

"Nila, Carmelita, Nancy, Ada, Belle, and Vivian."

"How? Where?" Holten felt a shock of loss almost as intense as when Amy first told him Preacher Smith had proposed. Of the twenty beautiful women Della Caldwell had brought west with her, sixteen had disappeared. "What did you lose them to?"

"To the worst pestilence known to madams," Della said.

"You don't mean . . . ?"

"Yes," the lovely madam confirmed, then ground the filthy word out between her lips with cold, angry eyes to keep it company. "Marriage."

"*All* of them?" Eli pressed.

"I don't know what the miners had," Della sighed with resignation. "All I can figure is those boys dragged their peckers on the floor when I wasn't looking."

A moment's silence welded their friendship once

74

again. Then Eli remembered his newly acquired friend and introduced Les Thacker. Della made him welcome.

"You've known this tail twister a while, then?" Les inquired of the madam.

"Yes. He once escorted my girls and I to Arizona. By the time he'd worked his way through the whole flock, he had to be carried to his horse each morning."

All three laughed heartily. In the silence that followed, Eli's words came softly.

"I just lost one of my own ladies to this malady you referred to."

"Oh, Eli, that is a shame. Let's have a drink," Della suggested as she signaled the bartender. "To love and affection at a fair price."

"How do you stay in business, Della?"

"It ain't easy," she answered. "I've lowered my standards and hired a couple of local girls, but I won't have no Mexicans or darkies working my customers. When those cowpunchers roll in here with their pockets stuffed with money and their pants stretched with lust, it's like owning a diner with a hundred hungry people waiting to be served and precious little to feed them."

"Sounds like hard times, Della."

"*Hard* times is when I'm supposed to be making money," Della countered.

"Hey, Holten," Thacker interrupted. "You taking me to the doc's or am I going to sit here till I'm healed up?"

"I'll be back," the scout assured the madam as he rose from his chair.

"I hope you don't mind if we reminisce a bit about old times?" Della smiled an invitation that had little to do with recounting the past, and Holten knew how all those cowpunchers felt.

The doctor peered over the top of his spectacles at

Holten, his patient sitting behind his back, the wound exposed and draining.

"You get a room for two days. I'm going to wash and dress this hole and I want to see him tomorrow and the day after."

"Two days?" Thacker cried. "We can't wait that long!"

"You got three dollars?" Dr. Doyle asked.

Eli fished three silver cartwheels out of his pocket. He held them out before the surgeon's face.

"Then you can afford to keep this boy healthy and whole," the doctor continued, taking the coins from Holten's palm. "Now you go to the boarding house up the street here, tell Mrs. MacMurphy that Dr. Doyle sent you and that you'll need a room for yourself and one of my patients. I can promise you she's much more reasonable in price than I am. The rooms are clean . . . hell! Spotless. And her cooking is above average. Go! I'll have someone bring this Texan up there when I'm done."

Following Doyle's directions, Eli went up the muddy morass of Broadway and entered the MacMurphy boarding house.

Mrs. MacMurphy, a large, rose-cheeked Irishwoman, glared at the scout.

"No swearing!" she started. "No drinking and most of all, no women!"

It all sounded vaguely familiar. With the room secured, Eli headed back out for the Good Times Saloon, looking for his destiny and fond memories.

Seven

Mike Howser, the bartender, recognized the scout from their long-ago acquaintance. He gave Holten a beer on the house and then Eli asked the inevitable question.

"Where's Miss Caldwell, Mike?"

The counterman looked deadly serious. "She's waiting for you, Holten. In her room."

Holten stared across the still sparse crowd in the saloon.

"What room number?"

"What else? Number one."

Eli nodded sagely, looked to the stairway, then left the half consumed beer as he started walking deliberately toward the steps.

"Take it easy, Holten," Mike warned. "She's been handling only the top dogs in the town. The mayor, the bankers, the cattleman's association. That's bound to make any woman . . . restless."

Holten stopped for a moment, wiped at his lips, looked back long enough to give the barman a silent nod of thanks, then started climbing.

Della Caldwell wore a lacy black lounging gown that slid across the thick rug that covered the hard oak floors of her room. She stood no more than five feet five inches, with large, firm breasts and a narrow waist. Thick, rich auburn hair swept up over small, pink ears into a fashionable style, with sausage-roll curls cascading down her back.

"Eli," she cooed demurely as she swung the door open invitingly. "Whatsoever a surprise."

Eli entered the pleasure palace to end all pleasures.

The floor had rugs practically from wall to wall. Red lace curtains filtered sunlight through the windows. A bed big enough for a whole family of sod-busters filled one corner of the room, a brass and black pot-bellied stove snuggled into the other side of the suite, and the washstand held a gold-plated pitcher and basin. The walls had more mirrors than wallpaper. The wallpaper was scarlet, with thick-flocked roses. Over the bed, more mirrors.

Eli realized his jaw hung loose. He snapped it shut, crinkled a smile to his lips. "Lovely place you have here, Della."

"Let's cut the small talk," the madam retorted in a strained voice. "I need a real man in the worst way. You want me. Surely something can be worked out."

"Della," Holten rebuked her gently as he closed the gap between them. "There's no reason to make this nasty."

Her hot breath sighed across the scout's neck as he wrapped work-hardened fingers behind her slim back.

"If I've offended you, darling, please forgive me."

"I plan to, Della, in just a little while."

The madam wrestled from his grasp and with a laughing, seductive smile, she stepped back to start pulling at the bows that held her silky wrap to her frame.

With a whisper of rustling clothes the woman disrobed. Her lush, full body and firm legs flushed blood and adrenaline into Holten's loins. A thick mat of auburn curls covered Della's passion-swollen mound at the juncture of her legs. Holten felt his staff swiftly rising in response to this glorious vision. He set to jerking the clothes off his body. They seemed to fly in all directions until his tall, gangly body became naked, and his wonderful wand of ecstasy stood erect and aching, stretching at the skin that held it together.

Eli rushed to the equally naked Della and, with both hands, he grasped her flaring hips and drew her closer until she struggled hot and moist against his taut stomach. They fell onto the large bed, wrestling like children on the velvet red covers. Quickly he explored her body, dropping his bronzed shoulders until his lips flamed across her undulating crotch.

With his long, probing tongue he parted her rosy fronds and lapped at her musky dew. Della stifled a squeal of delight with one small hand and ground her puffy cleft against his forehead. He continued to lick and thrust and consume her sweet nectar until the supposedly jaded madam could bear it no longer. Weak in the knees, she struggled from her prone position, getting to her hands and knees on the firm bed.

Eli swung into position behind her, gliding the curved length of his mighty prod along the feathery pink veils of her outer chamber, seeking that elusive node of pleasure that he'd heard called a "rabbit's nose."

The sensitive tip of his throbbing phallus contacted it; a small, bean-shaped button that extended into the top of her slippery passage. He began to thrust violently against it, swinging his hips in a circular motion.

Della moaned like a woman half her age and vibrated with ecstasy. Only a few times had she felt so wonderful, and it had been with an unnaturally gifted man many years before. She had been young and unsure of herself, he the older sophisticate who gently initiated her into the pleasures of unrestrained sex. She had dreamed of him, longed for him, ached in her bed for him even as other men struggled on her chest. Only Eli Holten could raise her to such heights of delight, and she rejoiced at his heavy presence deep within her.

Her heart began to palpitate and she felt her sanity fleeing from her in mountainous joy. Of its own accord, her canal began to contract in time with the powerful lunges that so destroyed her reason. If she had to die, let it be now. But first let her have more . . . more . . . more.

Holten continued to plow into her while a hot syrupy flow of delectable headiness washed over him. He felt the start of his gradual climb to oblivion and slowed the lady's frantic efforts, pacing it to draw the utmost in pleasure. Della lowered herself to her shoulders on the bed, to elevate her nether parts and allow him deeper penetration. In long, delightful tingling strokes he gladly complied, driving to the core of her womb and withdrawing to an accompanying lament of gypsy violins. Ever so sad a parting on each outward stroke, ever so blissfully thrilling on the inward plunge. All thoughts of Thacker and *Maman-ti* and Kiowa-Apache raiding parties fled his mind. He sought only to give and take all the joy he could endure.

When at last the explosive climax arrived, the writhing, straining couple took flight in mutual release to a pardise beyond mortal ken. Ten minutes later, with his heart rate barely slowed, Della's questing lips rekindled the fires in his loins. This time Holten lay back while Della tended to every desire with hand, mouth, and pulsing love pouch.

With the skill only years of excellent experience gives, she managed to ignite his blaze for three more excursions into the realm of unbounded pleasure. A pleasant day wandered into the night, and Eli only hesitantly pulled himself from the cauldron of lusty desires.

"I'll be leaving for the Panhandle as soon as I can," Eli explained as he donned his clothes. Della's auburn locks hung about her heart-shaped face as she absently stroked her firm breasts, working her red nipples as she spoke.

"If by chance, Eli, you come across a lady with truly fine character who's looking for pleasant labor, make sure you send her to me." She smiled as she adjusted her well exercised hips. "With these cowpokes and their gold on the hoof coming up the trail, there's a fortune to be made here in Wichita."

"Damn," Doyle cursed, staring under the bandages at Thacker's wound.

"What's wrong, doc?" Les asked. The surgeon gave the ranger a surly look.

"You're weird, boy."

Les perked up with the comment. "I'm a Texan, sir."

"Well, that might explain it."

"What's the problem, Dr. Doyle?" Eli pressed.

"Your partner's wound is just about healed," Doyle explained. "Yesterday I was worried about infection. Today I'm worried about whether I earned the three bucks I charged you." He looked at the young ranger with awe-tinged respect. He had no idea how to deal with a man who didn't need his services. "If he's not careful, he won't even have a scar to brag about."

"Then hell's bells, Holten, what are we waiting for?" the Texan sang. "We get our horses, round up some grub and start down the trail to the greatest state in the Union."

The scout had entertained thoughts of visiting Della a

few more times before heading out, but the Texas Ranger had a point. Time was wasting.

It felt good out on the open land of Kansas. It felt nearly as good in Indian territory when they crossed into it two days later. The flat stretches differed greatly from the familiar stomping grounds of Dakota, which Holten called home. Everything seemed sparser here. Instead of miles of green buffalo grass, nests of loco weed, horsetail, and plains larkspur burst from the hard-packed dirt. Only a few stunted oaks and solitary blackjack pines dotted the horizon. Everything looked drier, Eli thought; a strange view since a spring rain rushed over them twice and pounded the ground like bullets until it sloshed against their mounts' legs. Occasional watering holes appeared near the trail, their places well marked by the hoof prints of livestock.

The first herd the two travelers encountered marched two thousand strong, storming north with their invincible numbers, churning the wet ground into sticky mud, controlled, or at least attended to, by a handful of drovers.

Thacker seemed to instinctively seek out the chuckwagon, which required the two men to double back.

The driver of the wagon looked as crusty as bread, and Thacker approached him with the delicate charm Eli would have expected him to use pursuing a young woman of his choosing at a barn raising.

"Beautiful day," he volunteered to the armed rider on the box of the wagon.

"Good day for dying, if you've a mind to it," the surly little man with the white beard and long snowy hair countered. The shotgun in his lap pointed suggestively toward the two riders. His beady black eyes nervously flashed from Holten to Thacker and back to Holten again.

"I'm Les Thacker," the young Texan continued,

ignoring the wagon rider's hostile comment with a smile. "And this here is Eli Holten. He's chief scout for the Twelfth Cavalry, come down to do a little tracking for Captain Reagan, Frontier Battalion. I'm a Texas Ranger and I was looking to see if there's any news from the Panhandle you might have heard."

With the mention of the Texas Rangers, the shotgun-toting wagoneer noticeably perked up. "A ranger, ya say. Why didn't you speak right up, boy? I'm Frying Pan Jack, cook for this crew. Jim Dobie's herd. I'm gonna be setting up camp aways a piece. Hang with me and I'll feed you."

"Appreciate the offer, Jack," Les answered, "but we've gotta put some miles toward Texas."

"Then you best be damn careful, boys." Jack's eyes scanned across the two men. He looked as serious as when they first rode up. Now, however, he seemed concerned for them. "Kiowa-Apaches on the trail. They scattered Teddy Blue Abbot's herd all over the territory day before yesterday. Killed at least three of his hands."

"But I thought this was Cherokee country," Eli said.

"Damn straight." Frying Pan Jack huffed disgust. "Kiowa-Apaches in Cherokee land, raiding cattle. I ain't never heard nothing so queer in my life."

Thacker and Holten exchanged quick, nervous glances. The disease they'd come to cure, or at least diagnose, looked like it had spread out of the Panhandle.

"How many herds are on the trail?" Les asked.

"It's still early in the season, but I figure about five herds including our own, which is near as many as I've ever heard of on the trail this close together. It's gonna be a banner year for beef."

Les and Eli bade the cook good-bye, then turned toward the south and headed down the Chisholm Trail.

The lone rider traveled quick and cold down through

Indian territory. He avoided people, following the trail, yet staying out of sight. Lampbertson knew the scout and the ranger had to be behind him. He didn't want any cowpuncher or trail boss telling them that some character who matched his description had passed by. The gunslinger adjusted his shortened Colt .36 Navy on his hip and went to find Read, his boss.

The day grew late as Holten and Thacker came upon another chuckwagon, where a fat man wearing a black wool hat over his graying hair, with a spotless white apron over his Levis and flannel shirt, busily worked in front of the camp. As a meal cooked in nearby Dutch ovens, the cook's dogrobber brutally scrubbed pots, pans, and plates in a large tub. Suds and water splashed in all directions. From where he sliced potatoes into a big cast iron skillet, the old man looked up suddenly, spotting the two approaching riders. With a smooth step he hefted a Sharps .45-90 into his hands and slid toward the chuckwagon.

"Hey," Les cried and stood in his stirrups. "I know that old buzzard."

The man at the camp obviously recognized the ranger. His neck stretched up and his hunched posture straightened. The cook let the Sharps drop to one hand.

"Wild Man?" the oldster crackled out. "Is that you?"

"Dirty Dave!" Thacker shouted down. "I recognized you by your soap suds."

From a distance of nearly a hundred feet, Les dismounted and started walking his horse toward the waiting old man.

"Why we getting off so soon?" Eli asked, following the Texan's lead.

"Anyone who knows and likes Dirty Dave knows to not raise dust that might get on his pots and pans. Dave's

84

a great chuckwagon cook, but he's so soap and water crazy, so damn clean, that he's dirty."

"And that's why they call him," Eli started, then the two men finished in unison, "Dirty Dave."

"Wild Man, you're a sight for sore eyes," Dave greeted as Holten and Thacker entered the camp. Then the old cook studied Eli with one closed and one cocked eye. "Who's your friend?"

A quick introduction had Dave stretching a hand toward Eli. The scout noted his grasp was with the strength of the good and sincere.

"You boys planning to stay here the night?" Dave inquired.

"If it's all right with you, we could stand a mess of your sob stew."

"And a passel of my sourdough biscuits." Dave chortled like he was offering them a good drink or a horny woman. "Old Zeke Newman's N Bar herd is right behind me."

Eli looked to the south where the old man pointed and saw a large dust storm headed their way.

"The boys should be bedding them down soon. I was hopin' you'd stay." Dave leaned over and dropped his ragged voice. "We got Injun troubles, ya know."

Eight

The red-tinted sandstorm slowly grew into a giant herd of swarming cattle, with riders moving along its sides as though sucked up in the wind of the creatures' travel. While Eli and Les unsaddled their mounts, one rider out ahead of the herd rode to a slight rise, pulled his hat from his head and flashed it across his chest.

Instantly, four men, chaps and hats flapping in the breeze, peeled off and came careening toward the chuckwagon. At a hundred feet they veered off and came up on camp from downwind. Dirty Dave carefully studied their course. They leaped from their horses and ran toward the fire.

Holten noted that each man had a rifle, and some had revolvers stuck in their belts. He knew that, because of thunderstorms and the lightning that came with them, cowboys preferred not to carry anything metalic, like a firearm, unless they felt it absolutely necessary.

"Best you wash your hands before you even think of eating," Dave growled at the riders. "And *you*. Whoa!"

The cook pointed at the smallest and slowest figure, a youth with a coating of dust on him as thick as fur. The boy froze and looked out from under dirt-laden eyebrows.

"Yes, sir," he squeaked.

"You forgot to knock your hat clean. And while you're at it, take your coat off and beat it a bit, too. And, wash your hands *and* face."

"Yes, sir," the boy replied in a cracking voice. He retired to a respectable distance. There he removed his felt hat and started slapping it against his side. Dust rose from him.

"Drag riders." Dave said it like a curse. "Always the greenest, dumbest men in the lot."

"He's fourteen years old and right off the farm," one of the other riders remarked from the washtub as he scrubbed at his hands. "Next year he'll be riding flank."

"*If* he lives through this cattle drive," Dirty Dave shot back and, with a thrust of his bearded jaw and flash of glaring eyes, dared the swing man to say anything more in mitigation. Instead, the cowboy stared dutifully down at his hands as he washed them.

Les leaned toward Eli and whispered at him from the corner of his mouth. "Only a fool argues with a skunk, a mule, or a trail-herd cook."

The youth returned to the scrub bucket, hat beaten and coat removed. He scrubbed at his face and hands like his life depended on it.

"You boys standing on formality, waitin' for a written invite?" Dave shouted at Holten and the ranger. "Get over there and get in line."

Eli realized they'd been standing to one side, and, yes, they had been waiting to be invited. The surly Dirty Dave stepped to the scout's side and chortled. Holten got a place behind Les as the hungry men and the visitors waited patiently for the cook to start serving them.

"You're gonna love my son-of-a-bitch stew."

The cook laughed as he meandered toward the drop-table tailgate of the wagon. Dave carefully studied each man as he passed, walked to the front of the line, all the while checking to make sure their hands met his exacting approval. A few he seemed to nearly reject, but with a contemptable curl of his lips, he let them slide and reached the array of Dutch ovens that his dogrobber had brought from the fire pit.

"When I give you your stew, you go right over there and take no more than two biscuits." Dirty Dave pointed at a bucket on the side of the chuckwagon. With that he started ladling his stew out onto the waiting plates in front of him.

"We gotta eat and get back out there," one man in front of Thacker said to the man ahead of him.

"You rush Dirty Dave and we might have ourselves a 'Spanish supper,'" the man in front answered.

"Can't do that," the first cowboy decided. "I ain't got no more notches in my belt to tighten up."

"Dirty Dave is the most cantankerous crew cook in all of Texas," Les explained to Eli. "And he takes a heap of pride in that brand."

Thacker's turn came up quickly, although it seemed forever to Holten as his stomach started taking note of the good smells from the Dutch ovens wafting to his nostrils.

"I want all you boys to meet Les Thacker and his friend, Eli Holten," Dave shouted out as he dumped a hefty portion of a thick, brown stew on the Texan's tin plate. "He's a ranger an' Holten's a scout for the army, so y'all treat them like they were riding with you."

The four drovers grunted greetings to the two men while they stuffed their mouths. Up until then they'd ignored the guests in their quest for a hot meal. They received two—and only two—sourdough biscuits from the small keg where Dirty Dave had dumped them to keep the bread warm after he'd baked them to a golden flaky brown, then poured strong Arbuckle coffee into tin cups.

Eli sat down with his meal. Besides the strange sob stew, he had a mess of navy beans, some potatoes fried with onions, and the two biscuits, with a tin full of coffee. He dug a fork into the stew, took a careful bite, then felt a smile break across his face.

"Damn," he declared. "That's good stew."

The other men, including Les, laughed a bit at the surprised exclamation. Dirty Dave glared at the scout as though suspecting he was making a joke.

"What'd you expect, Yankee? Hot cow shit with piss gravy?"

"How do you make something like this? It's the best I've ever tasted." Eli jammed another mouthful of the stew into his face, speaking through the meal.

"You throw ever'thin' in the pot but the hair, horns, and holler," Dave growled.

"It's made from a yearling," Les explained. "One that's broke a leg or something on the drive. Its brains, tongue, liver, heart, sweetbreads, kidneys, lungs, and marrow gut all get cooked, plus Dave's special ingredients."

"I'll never tell," Dirty Dave challenged through a grin of pride.

Everyone turned to their food for long, quiet moments. Then Holten broke the silence. "Dave told us you've met up with some Indians," he remarked, turning his attention to the cowboys wolfing down their meals.

"Damn right," the drag man squeaked up. "We met up with the meanest passel of redskins this side of the Rio Grande, or my name ain't Shorty Deussen."

"Kiowa-Apache," the swing rider qualified. "About a dozen of them. I expect they're out there right now studying on us. Didn't bother us so much as they did Al Blocker's crew, right out behind us by a day's ride. Killed three of his drovers and scattered his cattle from here to New Mexico."

"Kiowa-Apaches?" Les asked. "They're awful far from their homes."

"You know that, and *I* know that," the cowboy retorted. "But I figure no one told them red niggers."

A rider charged up from the milling herd that seemed to fill the horizon to the south.

"What's taking you men so long?" the thin-mustached man shouted as he rode right into camp. Holten surmised that this must be Zeke Newman, owner of the N Bar Ranch, bossing his own trail crew. The only man who'd dare to raise dust in Dirty Dave's camp. The rider reined his horse and started pulling off his rawhide gloves.

The men jammed food into their mouths as quickly as they could.

"You're supposed to eat quick and get out there to relieve the other men. So damn well hurry."

"Don't rail on 'em so, Zeke." Dave stepped up to the boss's horse. "I've held them up. Dirty as hogs when they came in."

"Ain't got time for your usual lessons in manners, Dave. I think the herd's ready to run," Newman answered, brow creased with his real concern. The men froze in mid-bite, then redoubled their efforts.

"Did I hear him right?" Holten asked Les. "He thinks the cattle are going to stampede?"

"If cows get it in their minds to run, anything can set them off." Thacker nodded at his statement as he jammed another mouthful of Dave's sob stew between his teeth.

"We got guests, Zeke." The cook pointed at Eli and the ranger and introduced them.

"Glad you're here," Zeke greeted warmly and the scout could tell he meant it. "I got Indians trailin' us, a herd spooked for the sake of it, and damned if one of my point men isn't saying he smells a thunderstorm coming our way."

"No need to smell it, boss," the swing man offered as he jumped to his feet and stabbed the air with his fork to the southwest.

In the distance a line of dark clouds appeared near the horizon, eerily lighted by flashes of lightning. The tempest brewed so far away that Eli could not hear the thunder claps over the thudding hoofs of the milling herd.

"Damn," Newman growled. He turned to his cook. "Dave, I've gotta get the other men in here to eat before that thing hits."

"I'll be ready," Dave answered as he ran toward his second set of Dutch ovens. Then he made a magnanimous concession. "An' they won't have to wash up, ne'ther."

"You boys finish up pronto. I'm going to need every good man out there to keep the cattle bedded if we can. Start wheelin' 'em the minute you get out there."

Les jumped to his feet, finished up his stew in a gulp and started hustling for his horse.

"Where are you going?" Eli inquired.

"Same place you are, Holten," the young ranger answered as he lifted his saddle from where he'd settled it on the ground. "He said every good man, right?"

Holten quickly resaddled, following Thacker's lead.

"I rode with Shanghai Pierce when I turned thirteen," the ranger explained. "I'd still be pushin' cows up the trail, only my cousin Frank died while serving in the rangers, so I took his place."

The air turned ominously still and humid. Sweat started pouring down the cowboys' faces and stung their eyes as they walked their horses out to where the herd had begun to bed down.

They went directly to the left side of the gather,

leaving only one man on the right. The four men they relieved rode headlong toward the chuckwagon.

The cattle seemed settled enough to Eli. They rested, hipshot, as they munched the sparse grass, or sat with their legs tucked under them.

"If the cattle stampede, they'll naturally start favoring the right," Les explained.

"Then why aren't we on the right side?" Eli asked.

"If you think you're gonna stop them from going anywhere they want with anything short of a stone wall, you don't know cattle," Les chided. Holten felt like the drag rider, a kid, always asking stupid questions.

"The cattle go right," Thacker continued. "We just help them to go a little righter, until they're running a pinwheel. In a little while they'll start milling again and then we try to bed them down."

"How long does all this take?" Holten asked.

"All night."

"That's what I figured."

A heavy mist rose from the ground. Between the sweat in his eyes and the mist the scout had to strain to see Sonny's ears, which he counted on watching because they relayed warning signals.

The clouds menacingly closed on the herd. The flashes became brighter against their black backdrop, and the rolls of thunder grew louder, shaking the ground.

Suddenly, balls of electricity—St. Elmo's fire—played along the tips of the horses' ears and the steers' horns, leaping snakelike from tip to tip around the herd. The blue light wavered like a vision out of hell.

The cattle lowed, fear flashing through their tiny brains and turning their wide brown eyes mostly white. Some rose and the horsemen started riding out to quiet individual animals. Shorty Deussen began to sing in a thin, sweet soprano.

Eli looked up and it seemed to him the blackest and

biggest cloud hung right over their heads. Some of the riders returned from the chuckwagon and Holten considered that a good sign.

"It looks bad," Les cried out to Holten over the crashing of celestial artillery. It seemed to Eli that most of the herd still remained unmoved, resting where they stood or lay. Then a blinding flash of lightning suddenly fired stark white light across the countryside. One electric tendril shot out.

It fried a bare-limbed, lone tree near the edge of the cattle. With it, the wind whipped up and the temperature suddenly dropped twenty degrees. When darkness returned, redolent with the odor of ozone, it seemed a hundred times blacker. By the time the thunderclap finished its bass drum roll, the rumble of hoofs and the clatter of horns rose above the roar of the storm.

In Eli's eyes, it looked as if the cattle hadn't simply risen to their feet and then started stampeding, but rather they were on their feet which were already running and the next jump was into hell itself.

Sheets of rain swept over the terrified animals. Eli loosened his reins, wrapped both hands around his saddle horn and prayed Sonny knew where he was going. The Morgan took off after the longhorns like he'd done this all his life.

The pounding herd headed north. Off in the distance Eli could make out riders ahead, slapping at the leaders with their lariats, almost seeming to be driving them on. Then Eli sensed the herd make a slight shift to the right, hardly noticeable, but still favoring that direction. He reined Sonny in and backed off from the deadly horns that appeared to stab at him out of the darkness. Slowly he fell behind.

He didn't know what else to do. Why exhaust Sonny and himself? He pulled his poncho from off his bedroll and covered his head and shoulders. It looked like a long night.

Captain Reagan waited down behind a boulder that lay next to the road headed east from Dimmit, forcing the wagon trail to reroute itself around the huge rock. The officer hummed softly to himself until his ears heard an approaching wagon, then he looked to his left. One of his rangers took his hat off and peeked over the sage he hid behind. He glanced over to Reagan and nodded.

Leroy Barker had deigned to show up. Oh well, the Texas lawman thought to himself, better late than never. Duke Reagan hefted his Winchester into his hands, waited until he could hear the clatter of the wagon on the other side of the boulder, then stepped around it as Barker had to slow down to make the sharp turn.

With an effortless jerk, the captain chambered a round in his weapon and stepped up to the slow-moving wagon.

"Rein 'er in, Barker," Reagan ground out of his throat. Instantly, a dozen men surrounded the suspect trader.

"What's the meaning of this?" Barker demanded. Reagan felt a twinge in his stomach. The trader didn't look like he'd been caught at something illegal. "What are you rangers doing?"

"A rancher near the New Mexico border sent me a telegram," Reagan explained. "Said he saw you a week ago in Lincoln County loading up with rot-gut whiskey and maybe some stolen guns. Now, who'd be customers for such things?"

Reagan didn't wait for a reply. "Seems you got drunk in a whorehouse a few days later, headed this way. Told a little lady you had some fine toys for a bunch of *coup*-hungry Kiowas in the Indian territory. She told her boss and the madam sent word to me. Now you're a hell of a

95

long way from the Nations and headed the wrong way at that. Under the circumstances, I'd like to see what you have under that tarp."

Tom Meyers, the redheaded volunteer scout, leaped to the wagon box and started wrestling with the rope. Other men joined in and soon they dragged the covering back.

The wagon bed lay bare.

"I could'a told you that," Barker, a small, skinny man, announced in a wounded tone. A note of fear had slipped into his voice, the ranger captain observed. "I think you owe me an apology."

"Maybe . . . maybe not. First, tell me, Leroy, why would a trader be traveling all the way across the Texas Panhandle without something to sell?" Reagan turned away with disgust and kicked at a loose rock. Then he spun back, his face red with anger, voice harsh as a hardwood rasp.

"What *are* you doing here if you aren't doing some kind of business?"

Barker lost color in his face and a cold film of sweat stung his eyes. "T-there's no law against a man moseyin' about a bit, is there? My reasons for being here is none of your business. Am I under arrest? I want to know the charges."

"For selling guns and whiskey to the Indians!" Meyers cried in rage.

"No charges, Leroy," the captain countered coolly through a smile. "You're not under arrest. C'mon, boys, let's follow this road back and see if we can find Mr. Barker's lost goods."

"Let's bring him along," Meyers suggested, pointing at the trader.

Reagan thought on that for a moment. He doubted whether they'd find the weapons and firewater. Texas was a big place and a cache of guns could be hidden anywhere.

"No reason to bother this *honest* merchant," Reagan intoned sarcastically through a flood of gravel in his throat. "We'll say *adios*, Leroy. Just remember, the rangers are always watching."

The dozen men disappeared into the brush they'd been hiding in. Barker waited until he couldn't hear them anymore, then crawled off the wagon to try to catch his breath. His bladder pained him and he rushed frantically to open his fly and expose his stinging penis before he went in his trousers.

Gradually he calmed. He'd hidden his merchandise not more than three miles back, in a wash by the road. It would be impossible to find them, he knew, but still, it had been a close one. Word had gotten to him barely in time.

Nine

Eli knew something had to be wrong. He counted riders.

He had seen earlier that the crew consisted of eight drovers on this crew. Including himself and Thacker, the trail boss, and even putting the cook on a horse, there should have been at the most twelve riders. Even in the frequent flashes of lightning from the storm, the scout should not have been able to see all of them at once from his position at the back of the herd.

Holten counted fourteen and recognized only three. They all ran along behind and at the extreme flanks of the stampede.

With each blaze in the heavens, a pause in the rumble of hoofbeats would mark where the entire herd leaped into the air in unison and landed in a thud and then they all took off with new energy. After one such prodigious blast, the riders suddenly disappeared, gone with the cover of the new darkness. The clouds scudded away, whipped by violent winds in excess of sixty miles per hour, and the tumultuous front of the storm ran ahead of the stampede. Eli urged Sonny to longer strides and came up on the left of the cattle. He spotted Thacker's paint and veered up next to it.

"Indians!" the scout shouted over the hissing downpour and constant boom of runaway hoofs.

"Where?" Thacker asked.

"Behind the herd."

Les's eyes went wide, then they closed like the Texan's hard slash of a mouth and firm, clenched jaw. Eli knew the reason and spoke it aloud.

"Dirty Dave."

The two men peeled off. In the dark, Zeke Newman seemed to loom up in front of them, a Sharps rifle across his lap.

"Mr. Newman," Eli bellowed. "Indians!"

Newman, Holten, and Thacker headed toward the camp. Eli led the way. He followed the trail in the dark, spotting the unshod hoofprints of the war ponies in the fading flashes of lightning.

"They're making for the camp, that's certain," Eli announced.

Eight sets of horses turned to the east, three continued straight for the location of the chuckwagon. The three white men burst over a slope above the campsite and quickly reconnoitered the situation.

In the gloom, Eli could see that Dirty Dave stood on the seat of the wagon, swatting three red men with an iron skillet as they tried to drag him out of the vehicle. The improvised weapon gave off a bell-like note as it struck one Kiowa-Apache skull and the stunned Indian staggered backward. Both Les and Zeke let out rebel yells and charged down the hill, revolvers drawn and firing into the air.

The hostiles took one look over their shoulders, then ran off into the gloom. Behind them, the whites rode headlong into the camp. Dirty Dave still stood on the seat and cursed them, challenging the fleeing savages to come back and fight like men.

"You all right?" Newman asked.

"Why the hell didn't they shoot me dead?" the cook inquired instead of responding to the question. "They had plenty of guns."

"Probably wanted to count *coup*," Eli answered. "Or else they didn't want to get our attention while we were busy with those damned cattle."

"Why didn't *you* shoot them?" Zeke snarled at his cook.

"Because *you* an' all those coyotes you call cowboys took every blessed shootin' iron in the wagon."

Eli looked over at the Sharps Zeke Newman now glanced nervously down at and wondered if that carbine had been the one Dave had been holding when Thacker and he showed up.

"Boy, let me tell you," Dave pressed on. "Normally in a lightning storm you chuck every blessed piece of metal you own in the back of this wagon. But let an Injun show his face and all I got is a pan and a prayer."

A sudden idea occurred to Eli. "Where are your spare horses?"

"The remuda is east . . . of . . . here." Zeke pointed into the dark. "Have them on rope hobbles." Then the same notion took him. "Oh, goddamnit!"

"If these Kiowa-Apaches are anything like the rest of the Plains tribes, I imagine they *were* in rope hobbles." Holten straightened up and sighed. "We'd best see which way the raiding party is taking them."

In the distance, the thunderstorm warred in the heavens as War Moon rode into where the braves had left their extra horses. He sought to gather up their property and the guard they'd left on the white girl.

The Indian youth they had left to watch their goods leaned spread-eagled against a rock, his breechcloth in his left hand. Little Louise hunkered down in front of him on her hands and knees, sucking his springy young member to its roots. The slender-built boy trembled with his excitement and panted through slack lips as his time of completion approached.

"Red Pony!" War Moon rebuked in a sharp voice. "You were to watch the horses, guard the camp, not pleasure yourself with the Yellow Bush. You didn't even hear me ride up."

"She would not stop!" the youth gasped. "She started on me the moment you left. Could a man refuse such a gift when it is forced on him?"

"You are not a man . . . yet. You are a boy and boys always have stiff lances. You should be ashamed of failing in your task."

Red Pony dragged his hardened stem from Louise's mouth, although she struggled against disengaging. "I am sorry, War Moon."

The war chief threw himself from the back of his animal and grabbed the sex-crazed female by her blond hair. He jerked Louise to her feet and took her in his arms. As he carried her to her horse, she began to lick his chest. He grunted in disapproval of this frivolity during a dangerous raid and draped her over the sway-backed mount. Then he tied her arms and legs together under its belly and slapped her on her bare bottom.

"We must leave," War Moon told Red Pony.

Louise's dress remained hitched up over her shapely hips and War Moon absently pulled it down, noticing from this vantage point that the girl's cleft had become inflamed from much friction and she dripped a blending of honeyed juices freely. The lubricating fluid glistened off silky yellow pubic curls and oozed down her legs. Despite himself, the warrior felt the urge come to him

102

again. His lance rose, swelling painfully against his breechcloth.

Louise made pitiful mewing sounds in an attempt to entice the aroused Indians, man and boy, closer to her. Red Pony yielded and stepped in close to where her head hung down. Instantly her tongue flicked out and inscribed delightful spirals on the sensitive surface of his exposed tip. A delirious shock jolted through the youngster and then he jerked himself away with a small whine of mortification.

Red Pony's face flamed with humiliation that he had succumbed so weakly and readily in the presence of his war leader. War Moon wanted to howl with frustration. The white girl would be his death, he thought. No, she would be the deaths of all of them.

All told the N Bar Ranch had rounded up twenty stray horses, and Zeke Newman scowled at the poor showing, now confined inside a rope corral.

"That ain't no remuda," the trail boss stated. "We're gonna have to go after those Indians or else I'm gonna have to sell my saddle."

The men looked at each other gravely. No one took that threat lightly from a man like Zeke Newton.

"We'll have to leave right away," Thacker stated.

"We can't track them at night," one of the cowboys argued.

"Of course we can," Eli answered back. "I can read sign anytime I have to. I just hope we have enough spare horses. We know they have plenty."

"Those cattle are gonna get up tomorrow and start moving out with or without us, on horses or not." The one point man stepped forward. "We better get those *caballos* and pronto."

103

"But," Shorty Deussen squeaked up, "when do we sleep?"

"Boy," Zeke answered gravely, "if you want to be a drover, you're gonna have to do your sleepin' in the winter."

"We're going to have to leave enough men to tend to the herd until we get back. Hughey and Logan, you try to nursemaid those doggies. We're taking the extra ponies, so go easy on the mounts you've got. You'll each need a night owl and one change for daytime. We'll be back with the rest as quick as we can."

"That'll make eleven of us to twelve of them," Eli figured out loud. "It's going to be one hell of a fight."

"Don't be silly, Holten," Thacker retorted. "These boys is Texans. Everyone knows one Texan is worth ten redskins in a fight."

The other men nodded sagely at the ranger's statement. Eli suppressed a groan.

War Moon sat on his blanket, propping himself up on his woven reed backrest as he watched the white girl's breasts bob in his face. He gasped for air and wondered if his pole would ever be the same again. He doubted it. It ached and tingled, yet with Yellow Bush around, it never seemed to slacken. At the moment, he could not even check to be sure it still existed. It lay buried deep inside Louise's ever eager pouch.

They had not intended to stop until morning, but their prisoner had amazing means for getting her way. She squelched a cry of joy and redoubled her gyrations, rocking her hips from side to side, squeezing her tits into War Moon's face.

A surge of life substance, a commodity in great shortage in the loins of the war party, burst with fresh

104

vigor from War Moon's pulsating shaft, then faded quickly into a feeble seep.

Little Louise leaped at the warrior's discharge. The two figures gasped for breath, the white girl with pleasure, the red man with a growing sense of desperation.

"You've been so good to me," Louise cooed at War Moon. "No one has ever let me have enough before. They all wanted to quit just as I started having fun."

Her eyes left the exhausted form below her and traveled hungrily around the impromptu camp among the rocks, eyeing each nervous warrior. They seemed spooked like the cattle had been by the lightning, afraid of being struck by her stormy passion. She pulled a blanket around her shoulders as she raised herself off the quickly fading red wand. It kept the cold from her back as she continued her search. Louise had not finished for the night. She still ached for satiation and had such a lovely collection of shapes and sizes to choose from.

Despite their exhaustion and the debilitating effects of the raid, the warriors' tired, aching organs stirred as the nude, white she-demon began to seductively rock and sway. She slid a hand up from her steamy crotch, across her flat belly and upward to cup her firm breasts, one at a time, then back down to her juicy cavern. All the while she uttered little grunts of delight and shuddered deliriously as she reviewed in her mind every brave and his endurance.

"Come on, boys," she panted. "I've heard so much about how you Injuns like to ravage us white girls. I've dreamed about it for so long. Since I was a little girl. Now you're here to do it for real. Hurry!"

Red Pony could not stand it any longer. The fourteen-year-old didn't understand a word the prisoner said, but her gyrations and cooing boiled his blood. He felt such fatigue that his legs wobbled under him. Five times he had coupled with her since before the sun rose that morning, not counting the three times she took him in her mouth. No boy in the village could release his sap so many times in one day, he thought with pride. Only so much of it made his stomach ache and his head feel dizzy. Still, the white girl stirred a primal urge he had to sate again . . . and again. He stumbled to the she-demon and wrapped his arms around her inside the blanket. Already his small member had stiffened to its greatest length. Louise responded with a shower of kisses on his neck and chest as he pressed its hot firmness against her bare flesh.

Shortly, they fell to the ground, while the other warriors watched. The boy entered her in a rush and she felt a special kind of delight she encountered only with him. She wanted him more than all the others combined. Yet Louise had every intention of laying with every warrior there that night, one after the other. Seconds if they wanted some.

The eleven riders checked their weapons, their ammunition, and the food that Dirty Dave packed for them. Holten had run out a distance to the south and now returned at a gallop. He dismounted, checked to make sure Sonny hadn't gotten winded in the night's stormy run, then turned to Zeke.

"Found their trail," he announced. "They've got about a hundred horses with them. There's thirteen of them now, but a couple are awful light. It might be squaws for making meals and the like, or young boys on their first fling at the warpath. They've got almost a two-hour jump on us."

"Hold it." The young ranger raised a hand. "Let me get this straight. You spotted thirteen horses with riders mixed in with a hundred other mounts, can say a couple was lighter than the others and did all this in the middle of the night?"

"General Corrington told your captain I was good," the scout modestly answered. "General Corrington's an honest man."

The party of drovers, led by Eli and Les, took off, headed south, and picked up the trail right where Holten said they would. The scout started noticing something strange an hour after they began their pursuit.

The war party had stopped for a short time, not quite an hour, Holten surmised, and there seemed to be a great deal of thrashing on the ground. Grass lay bent and flattened in several places.

"Think maybe they're sick?" Les asked.

"More likely drunk," Zeke suggested.

Eli scratched at his two-day old stubble. "If they got this drunk, I would think they'd have passed out right here."

"How far ahead of us are they now?" Zeke asked.

"No more than an hour, give or take some."

"No man can be that sure about signs," Les countered. Eli smiled.

"You care to lay a bet on that, ranger?"

Thacker didn't take the offer.

Two hours later Eli came on another thrashed grass scene. Though they had been making good time, the Indians had stopped again. Some of the things he spotted made Eli wonder about the cause of the halt. This time the raiders didn't leave for over an hour.

"At this rate, we'll catch up to them by morning," Eli stated.

The sun still had to crest the hills to the east, but in the false dawn, War Moon could see the white she-demon languidly curling from her blanket as she dismounted another one of his warriors. She had been through them twice that night that he knew of. The great war chief

107

realized he faced extinction if he didn't kill the white girl. Surely the white men with the *Wo-hahs* would pursue them. War Moon had even counted on it, in hopes of killing more of them. If the demon stayed among his braves much longer, though, the Kiowa-Apache war band would not have the strength to defend itself.

"We must rid ourselves of this monster," young Red Pony whispered to his leader, as if reading War Moon's mind. The boy's face was pallid and his voice shook slightly. Dark rings, like those on most of the older warriors, had begun to show under his eyes.

"Now I realize that this is why the white men in the rolling wood gave her to us," War Moon hissed.

"My lance hurts. It feels like it was on fire."

"Mine, too," War Moon admitted.

He pulled his knife out of the sheath, one he had taken from a pony soldier as a young man, and approached the girl.

Louise Van Pelton had found heaven. Twelve handsome red men, with twelve red rods to jam between her legs and make her tickle all over. The thought of it made the young nymph salivate in more places than her mouth. For eight years now she had tried to stuff herself with the one thing she most loved in the world, only to have them go soft on her and shrivel up. She had ached from the need of it from her earliest memories. Louise didn't know she suffered from an ailment incorrectly diagnosed during the Middle Ages as one form of possession by demons. She only knew that she thought of nothing else, wanted nothing else, actually doubled over in pain if she got no relief. Three years ago, when she had been caught with two of her brothers by her parents, she had been severely whipped and driven from her home.

Abandoned and desperate, she had used her only commodity to provide some form of survival. Her eagerness and youth frightened many men who could have cared well for her and she always seemed to go hungry. But not with these boys. The Indians seemed always ready to scratch her special itch and they fed her well. It kept her energy up for the long nights . . . and days . . . of delirious satisfaction. She stretched on her blanket and let the cold moist morning air chill her flesh. Goose bumps covered her and her nipples hardened with the cold. The one Louise knew as the leader suddenly stepped over her, a knife in his right hand.

Louise's affliction saved her life then. She felt the familiar hunger grow like a brush fire and she gasped, feeling a gush of hot liquid in her lower parts. Her breath became shallow and before the warrior could bend down, she sprang at him.

In the last few days, the white girl had learned how to get the savages' clothes off with ease and grace. She slipped under the binding cloth and, with a gulp, took War Moon's flaccid penis into her mouth. Her hands ran up his muscular rump, then back down to his scrotum, which she teased and fondled in a familiar way. With rapid strokes, her tongue rasped over the spongy tip, sending happy signals up through his body. His flesh arrow burst to life again, snaking down her throat and fulfilling her every thought and dream. Her ardor grew to a point of hysteria.

War Moon's passion grew in equal volume. He suppressed a scream as for a moment he believed the demon would suck his manhood off his body. Yet he couldn't bring himself to end her marvelous ministrations.

"As soon as she is done, I will cut her throat," the war chief promised and the other warriors took heart as the raving creature increased the urgency of her magnificent tugging.

War Moon fell to his knees, weak and shaken by the intensity of her efforts, convinced she would rip his weapon from his body. He quaked with exhaustion, even as he vibrated with excitement.

"Someone must distract her," he cried. "Red Pony, you who are my brother, take her with the vigor of your youth. You must save us all."

Red Pony hesitated, loathing to penetrate the hungry pit again. His small organ ached and felt raw in patches. His brother had called on him as a brother and a warrior, however, and he fell between the girl's legs from behind, even as she wrestled to get more of War Moon down her throat. Despite his apprehension, he thought ruefully, his own shaft stood at a hardened attention.

For a moment, Red Pony's penetration distracted Louise, though not long enough for War Moon to escape. The wild creature sucked him down to his side and shortly the warrior lost his sensibilities and rode the oral excursion to his completion. Now the demon let him go.

And one of the other warriors, though he knew what strength the strange white girl could sap from him, took War Moon's place. Louise greeted him greedily with a lapping tongue.

"Enough!" War Moon cried after the last warrior had sated his lagging urges in either or both of her willing openings.

To his amazement, Louise seemed to have had her fill. Exhaustion, or perhaps merely a need for sleep, finally left her quieted and sedate. She lay flat on her stomach, her legs bowed on the blanket she rested on.

The war leader called up the last of his strength, stepped to the white girl and leaned over her back. She languidly elevated her rump, looking forward to receiving them all in this position. Instead, War Moon fell to her side, grabbed her hair to keep her from struggling, then slipped his knife under to slit her throat open.

At that moment, a great white owl came screeching from the heavens. It snatched a scurrying field mouse off the ground no more than six feet away, then bounced back into the air, skimming over War Moon's head.

All of the warriors fell back and stood silent for a long time.

"It must be a sign," one brave volunteered finally.

War Moon sheathed his knife. "*Tejan*, the great owl prophet, was said to speak to an owl and be able to forecast the outcome of battles. Red Owl has talked to owls as well. Perhaps this creature was sent to tell us something."

"The Yellow Bush demon is a test of our manhood," Red Pony declared with youthful pride in the challenge. He pointed at Louise. "We are not to kill her. She is a test of our cunning."

"My little brother has truly seen a vision," War Moon declared.

From a hill to the north, Eli studied the herd of horses with field glasses. After two careful swipes he saw the naked, alabaster girl lying under a deeply bronzed warrior who pumped away with slow, but forceful strokes. Eleven other Indians stood about, re-hitching or removing their clothing.

"That's a white woman they have with them," Holten announced with alarm.

A moment of terse words and anger and the cowboys remounted with dispatch. Now they had a better reason than horses to pursue the savages.

Ten

War Moon spotted a flash of light from the north. With eyes trained from many years of stalking and being stalked, he could see the white men on the hill.

"We are being watched," the war chief shouted and, despite their strength being spent to the breaking point, the Indians sprang to their feet.

"I have a plan," War Moon announced as he glanced around the terrain to the south. He spoke quickly and concisely, giving each man a mission. With as much enthusiasm as they could muster, the braves split up, giving a tired war whoop.

The eleven cowboys came off the low grade and made directly for the war party and the stolen horses. Before they could get close enough, however, the Indian force split in two. The herd of horses headed off southwest, seven braves urging them on, a cloud of dust raised to confuse their pursuers. War Moon and four other braves, including Red Pony and Cold Wind, along with Louise, headed southeast. A rocky hill split the two bands from each other. The dust storm raised by the remounts billowed up on the small mountain's sides.

The cowboys reined up for a moment.

"We gotta go after the girl," Thacker cried and most of the riders nodded agreement.

"We have to get those horses first," Zeke argued. "Without the remuda, we're all going to have to walk to Wichita and I won't be able to pay you a cent."

"We can't leave the lady." Everyone looked back at Shorty Duessen, who stood up in his stirrups. "That wouldn't be right."

"Shorty and one other man will go after the woman with me," Eli decided the issue. "The rest of you run down the horses."

The other drag rider, a young man called Booger, raised his hand to volunteer.

"Let's go!" Thacker cried and the white men split into two groups.

The rocky hill and the dust raised by the horses hid the three warriors who peeled off from the horse herd, cutting across and heading to join War Moon.

The leader of the Kiowa-Apache party looked back over his shoulder and saw three white men pursuing them. He had hoped for maybe one or two more. Once they had dispatched these three, though, they'd swing around behind the whites chasing the horses and wipe them out. The warrior headed for a clump of rocks.

Eli led the way, the brim of his hat pinned to the crown from the speed of the wind. Shorty slapped heels against his mount and tried to keep up. Booger, on a fresh mount and proving to be a fine rider, ran to Eli's right. The scout glanced over in time to see the young drag rider bolt from his horse and strike hard. The cowboy fell under the hoofs of his mount, then rolled away behind.

The report of the rifle that had killed Booger followed.

Eli looked to his rear and to the right to the three Indians charging up to his side. A trap, the scout thought, and it had sprung full force on him and the two inexperienced youths with him.

Shorty Duessen jumped from his mount with his Spencer .50-56 in hand even as his pony got shot out from under him. The youth ran to a patch of larkspur and Johnson grass. One warrior headed toward the youth.

Eli slid down one side of Sonny, hooked his spur into the off edge of the saddle and fired his Winchester under the neck of the Morgan at the two braves still closing on him. The Sioux, who had raised him as a boy, had taught him this technique and it surprised and confused the Kiowa-Apache warriors.

The first Indian caught a round in the center of his chest. Blood exploded from between his shoulder blades out of an ugly, ragged exit wound. Like a circus acrobat, the warrior rolled off the back of his pony and disappeared in the dust.

Holten jerked the cocking lever so that the expended round jumped from the breech. He slammed it shut and the next round chambered in. The scout didn't even attempt to aim for the rider with his next shot.

He squeezed the trigger of the weapon as he chose the larger target offered by the pursuing Indian's mount. With a wild scream, the pony collapsed instantly and the red man flew over the head of his fatally injured pony. He slid along the ground across sand and gravel that tore at his bare flesh.

Eli regained his seat in the saddle and saw that the Indians with the white woman he had been chasing had dismounted in a cluster of rocks that Sonny stoutly charged. With a slight pull at the reins, the scout's mount changed direction, slowed down and headed to the left of where the hostiles had taken cover.

Sonny dashed in between a pile of sun-bleached white boulders. Eli reined the animal in and dismounted.

Quickly the scout calculated his situation. An unknown number of Kiowa-Apaches lay to his right. Shorty Duessen hid in some grass a hundred feet away to the left, fighting with at least one warrior, and anyone else that might be of help chased a herd of horses west of him. Quickly the scout pulled his Oglala Sioux moccasins from his saddlebags.

Eli hoped Shorty would be all right as the scout slapped his mighty beast on the rump and took cover in the jagged limestone. Sonny ran out onto the flat.

Holten crawled up into the boulders, maneuvering deeper into their cover all the time. He angled to work his way toward where he figured the hostiles had the woman. He'd come for her and didn't intend to leave her to the war party. It would surely mean her death.

The rugged stone cluster opened into a six-foot wide slit. Sand on the ground promised Eli the silence he'd hoped for to sneak up on the Kiowa-Apache warriors. White lumps of erosion-polished limestone rose to form walls on both sides. Holten leaned his Winchester against the rock wall and bent to start working his boots off and slip on his moccasins.

A blood-drenched scream tore out above him. Eli twisted to look up to his right. One fast moving brave hung in midair, closing the gap between the white man and himself with a slashing metal blade, decorated with the tassles of the warrior's soldier lodge.

With no time to spare, Holten ducked the murderous knife and slipped under it as the attacker sailed over him.

The scout's bowie knife appeared in his hand. As the Indian flew by overhead, Eli raked his blade evenly along the brave's belly.

Out poured blood and internals. The small and large intestines spiraled out and slapped the dusty ground.

116

Steam rose from the entrails in the sharp morning air.

Before the body of the mortally wounded brave hit the ground, Holten heard, then saw, another screaming red man charging him. The Kiowa-Apache ran down the length of the rocky slit. He jumped over his brother and stabbed at Holten with a murderous thrust of his war lance.

With a twist the scout dodged the chipped flint tip of the five-foot spear and realized why they hadn't shot him. They all hoped to count *coup* on him first. He couldn't help but think, though, that the Indian's attack lacked something. Energy or determination, perhaps.

Eli didn't have time to consider the phenomenon. He grabbed the lance and jerked at the bronzed warrior. Holten's tug pulled him past, so that the Indian stumbled beyond the white man, with a sharp kick to the groin to slow his aggressiveness. Holten slapped his blade into his antagonist's back, punched in between the second and third rib on the warrior's left side. This brave, too, got on with the business of dying.

Only he took the scout's bowie knife with him.

Blood from the first warrior had soaked Eli's arm and knife hand. Then the blade hung up in the clinging pulp of the second Kiowa-Apache's lung, and Holten felt the handle slip as the fatally wounded man went slack. Holten lost his grasp as the walking corpse reeled away from him. The red man twisted in his agony and the hilt jerked from Eli's hands.

A third warrior appeared and Holten recognized this one as the man he'd seen standing over the naked body of the white girl.

War Moon dropped screaming from the top of the rock face, slashing with his knife on the way down. Holten dodged the swings as he wrestled out his Remington. He wished he could "fast draw" like the killer on the train as his new assailant landed a solid blow to the scout's jaw.

Dazed for an instant, Holten's nerveless fingers dropped the revolver. War Moon followed up with a slash.

The scout rolled with the punch and parried the knife with his left forearm. He let the warrior's momentum throw him away from the danger. Another stab with the blade, only this time, Holten was ready.

The deeply bronzed, muscled arm with the knife hurtled forward and, for a split second, got overextended. Eli dodged and slipped the blade-wielding hand under his arm. As the scout twisted, he slapped his side against the warrior's elbow, locking it in place. Like a twirling battering ram, Holten dragged War Moon around and slammed the bent-over red man's head into a fourth warrior's solar plexus with enough force to send both attackers into a heap.

War Moon didn't suffer this indignity and then fall away emptyhanded. With the clearheaded effort of a leader and the Herculean strength that marked a true warrior, he reached out and grabbed Eli's revolver by its barrel. Even as a wall of hard muscled flesh and bone slammed into the top of his head and scattered his thoughts to the winds, he held on to that iron tube.

Eli stood staring at his reliable .44 in the hand of his enemy for only an instant before turning quickly to run to where he'd left his repeater. Another warrior stood in his way, brandishing a knife. He made a threatening stab at the scout, more to intimidate than to try to score a strike. Holten saw his chances of survival fading quickly.

All the time, though, something about these braves nagged at his consciousness. His attackers seemed . . . tired? Sick? Maybe a hangover haunted their skulls and weakened their fighting prowess. Yet he had not come across any discarded whiskey bottles. Eli hunkered down and braced for the next, and certainly the final, assault. At any moment he expected the crashing pain of a bullet from his own six-gun.

Instead of firing, War Moon and the two remaining warriors stumbled to the farthest end of the clearing. They faced the white man warily, obviously impressed with Holten's fighting ability.

War Moon could only marvel at how badly his well-planned ambush had gone. At that moment his six braves should have been taking the scalps off the three white men who had followed them and be readying to pursue the other whites to kill them as well. Instead, War Moon stood facing one single fighter who had killed three of his men. The battle had occupied them for so long the other warriors probably had to break and run, abandoning the horses.

Little Yellow Bush's powerful magic caused their troubles, robbed them of their strength, War Moon decided. Not only that, the white man before them fought like an Indian.

"You are a warrior, white man. Much power," War Moon admitted out loud in accented English. "You fight well. You fight like one of the People. Where did you learn this?"

Eli looked to his right and left. No escape. War Moon and his men had gathered their wits and weapons. They only waited for their leader to give them the word to kill him. If the scout made a run for cover, they'd finish him even before that. Holten had to bide his time. He straightened and spoke in a haughty voice.

"I am Tall Bear, son of Two Horns of the Oglala. From a young boy I was raised as one of the Dakota. I am a warrior of the Beaver Lodge and it is a good day to die."

The Kiowa-Apache grunted approval of the white warrior. They also felt relief that a common white man had not bested them thus far. Satisfied with the answer, War Moon thrust Holten's Remington into his war sash. Then a spark of cunning genius lit the savage's thoughts and a smile tugged at his stoic lips.

"Tall Bear is a great warrior," War Moon intoned, his gravelly voice tinged with awe—and desperation.

He turned to one of his braves and spoke quickly in their tongue. Then, as the warrior ran off, the party's leader turned back to the scout.

"You have fought well today. We are filled with pride in our brother from the sacred Black Hills."

Eli stood frozen as the red man approached him, his pistol in the war chief's beaded belt. The brave reached out with his left hand and rested it on Holten's tensed shoulder.

"Let us speak in peace, Tall Bear," War Moon continued. "I am War Moon, leader of this party, a Kiowa-Apache warrior and follower of Red Owl."

Holten remained unmoving, his face locked in a glower.

"We have no quarrel with the Oglala," the Kiowa-Apache stated. "Why do you ride against us?"

"I come for the woman," Holten demanded flatly.

"She means nothing to us." War Moon crossed his arms. "Is she of your family? Does she mean something to you?"

"I only know that you are a war party," Eli answered. "I know that you might take a white woman hostage, but you will not keep her. You will kill her soon."

"We have no war with the Sioux," War Moon repeated. "I can only see your fighting spirit."

The brave that the chief had sent off returned, dragging a blond-haired girl behind him, tossing her at War Moon's feet.

Eli noticed the leader step back, the slightest hint of revulsion on his face.

"My warriors and I wish to give the great Tall Bear a gift."

While War Moon spoke, the other warriors gathered up their slain comrades. One pulled Eli's blade free of the

120

body it was stuck in, wiped it on his leggings and handed it over to his leader.

War Moon gave the bowie, hilt first, to Holten, then handed the white man the Remington revolver.

"Your shoot-all-day is behind you. As well as this, we give you the woman. We have named her Little Yellow Bush, for her, ah, hair. We want only peace with the Oglala."

The other warriors already fell back into the rocks, disappearing even as War Moon began walking backwards away from Holten.

"Let us part as friends, Tall Bear."

The Kiowa-Apache vanished, leaving the strangely quiet white girl and Holten alone on the blood-stained sand.

The scout first gathered his rifle. He checked his weapons quickly, then gingerly scooted to the side of the young girl lying quietly on the sand.

Holten knew something didn't ring right and he watched the top of the rocks for an ambush. The hostiles should have killed him. Great respect for his fighting abilities would only have made his death more important to them. The girl turned her face to him. He knew that, though young, she had too many years behind her to have been kept to be raised as an Indian. She should have been killed shortly after being captured and raped.

A tear in the girl's dress top exposed one of her pink nipples, tight and hard. With the cold, Eli thought. He pulled his buckskin shirt from his shoulders and threw it over the girl.

Louise Van Pelton looked up at her rescuer and smiled. Holten noticed a certain desperation in her eyes, perhaps even . . . hunger.

121

Eleven

The Texas Ranger campsite at Las Moras Creek had become a permanent position for Captain Reagan. Tents had been pitched and a makeshift mess hall constructed under a tarp. Reagan had sat down a moment earlier under that tarpaulin to eat some lunch when the guard cried out.

"Rider comin' from the east."

"Who's it look like, Jethro?" Reagan inquired, his bellow sounding like a blast of gravel and dust.

"Looks a whole lot like Marshal Wharton, Cap'n."

A short time later, a big-bellied man, holding tenaciously to the reins of a mule, came trotting along the well-worn trail from Menardville into the rangers' camp.

"Duke!" the rider cried. "Bad news!"

"Hold it, Dorsey, old boy," the captain countered with a smile, his chuckle sounding like someone walking on pebbles. "Get inside my tent." He glanced around at his men, noting their concern.

His boys had been through a lot in the last few months.

Men of vision, men of honor, Reagan thought. Brave to a fault and fearless to the last man. The last ninety days hadn't been normal. Before Red Owl, they had met their opponents straight on and, win or lose, they got their licks in.

Fighting shadows and arriving always too late with nothing to follow had taxed the rangers of Company D's sense of invincibility, which every Texan held as sacred. In a moment of crisis, when they could be demoralized by whatever bad medicine they came up against, he didn't plan to have public discussions of more discouraging news, especially with the high-strung marshal of Menardville.

Duke Reagan ushered the profusely sweating lawman into his private tent. Wharton rushed to a crude chair in front of the captain's makeshift table made from planks across stacked ammunition crates. He fanned himself with a piece of paper he had crushed in his hand and sucked for air.

"Don't just sit there, Dorsey. Tell me what's got you so riled."

"Word just came from Fort Sill in the Nations," Dorsey Wharton gasped. He smoothed out the paper in his hand and gave it to the ranger.

Reagan sat on his sleeping cot, taking note of the date in the corner. Only a week ago.

"Says here Indians are raiding the Chisholm Trail. That's out of my jurisdiction, Marshal, you know that. Besides, Comanches and Kiowa kicking up their heels is nothing new."

Wharton gulped in a mouthful of air before bursting out his next line.

"Kiowa-Apaches, Duke. Not Comanches or Cheyenne or any of the civilized tribes. And they aren't kicking up their heels, stealing a couple of horses or getting some cattle for meat. They're killing people!"

124

The captain read on, seeing a picture get painted by the cryptic note from the commander of Fort Sill. The news grew grimmer with each line.

"He wants you to send Texans against those bastards, that's what!" The marshal of Menardville had caught his breath and now nodded at his own uttering. His jowls shuddered with his intensity. "Texans can go where no Yankee soldier-boy could even imagine."

"Ah, come on, Dorsey." Reagan curled his lips with disgust. "You rode with the Texas First Cavalry for the Union. That makes you as much Yankee as they are. Don't tell me those boys can't fight."

"Not like a *real* Texan, Duke," Wharton insisted. He looked into a corner of the tent and seemed to see far beyond it. "We Texans, we feel things those others don't. We fight for something different, maybe something better. We got a dream for a lot of great things . . . even things we don't understand." The town marshal looked back at Reagan and he felt embarrassed. "Aw, you know what I mean, don't you, Duke?"

The captain knew. No people in the country, not Yankee nor Southern warrior, had more of a sense of purpose, of . . . history, than Texans and, especially, the Texas Rangers. They knew they blazed a trail for others to follow, sacrificed for things that couldn't be touched or tallied up on a bank sheet, but deeds and ideas that would not be forgotten, ever.

"I'll be damned if I go riding off into the Indian territory. I have no authority. It's out of my jurisdiction, federal land. Besides, from what it says here, there's no Texans to be protected."

"They hit an XIT herd three days ago just north of the Texas line." Dorsey Wharton leaned on Reagan's table. "I'm supposed to ride out to Palo Duro Canyon and tell Charlie Goodnight four of his best hands got killed."

"That's not in this note," Reagan disputed.

"It's a fact, Duke, just the same."

The ranger captain handled the letter from the army for a few seconds more, thinking about what had come to him. The Kiowa-Apaches who had plagued him now seemed to have slipped into a place he couldn't touch, yet even now, they killed the people he swore on the Bible to protect. Charlie Goodnight owned the XIT Ranch, the largest in America, probably the world. Everyone liked tough, profane, cantankerous old Charlie. Reagan smiled grimly. The ranger no doubt knew the dead men personally. One of his favorite and most promising fighters, Les Thacker, rode somewhere on the Chisholm Trail, and had probably gathered a great deal of intelligence on what the Kiowa-Apaches were doing. And if Eli Holten proved to be half the tracker old Corrington said the man could be, the two of them might be on the scent right then.

"You're headed for Palo Duro Canyon then, Dorsey?" Reagan asked. The marshal nodded. "Could you stop by Tom Meyers's place and tell him to catch up with us? Me and the boys are going into Indian territory."

Holten stayed well hidden for more than three hours, carefully scouting the rocks until he assured himself War Moon had left.

The Kiowa-Apaches had not only fled, they'd abandoned a horse, with several bags of good Arbuckle's coffee, flour, and sugar. Only after being sure that the warriors didn't lurk in ambush did Eli wander out into the open.

First he found Sonny. The roan Morgan stood not more than two hundred yards away from the rocks, hiding in a bramble bush that tore at the great animal's flesh, though it offered some concealment.

The scout gently led the skittish horse safely out of the

thorns, checked to see if Sonny's wounds amounted to much, feeling that the care of his horse far outweighed that which Holten thought to give himself.

"All right, boy," Eli told his mount. "You're doin' fine. Let's see how Shorty's gettin' along."

Shorty Duessen had done the best he could. He lay face up in the cover he'd sought, a Kiowa-Apache war lance sticking out of his chest. He would never see fifteen. His eyes stared out directly where a brave's body lay, a .50 caliber lead slug in the chest quickly shortening the red man's life.

The warrior stretched out on the open flats, dragging himself in a straight line away from where the young cowboy lay murdered. He spit up blood as he slid through the Johnson grass, trying to find his mount.

Holten stood a few steps behind the dying warrior. He hesitated for a moment, then reached down with the tip of his Winchester and counted *coup*.

Ike Lampbertson moved slowly from the fire he'd made to prepare his noontime meal, rising to his full six-foot height, keeping his hands away from his gun. The redskins to his right carried enough firearms to bury him in a lead tomb. Every single weapon pointed at the shootist.

The gunslinger figured this surely would be his final resting place, minus his scalp. Ike hoped that any piece of his anatomy that the warriors wanted for mementos might be removed after he'd died.

War Moon hefted his Sharps carbine and relished the thought. A mere piece of lead would bring a bull buffalo back to the range. How much simpler this would be than the last ordeal.

They had killed many white men since starting out on Red Owl's raid. Many new scalps graced the warrior's *coup* sticks. Yet a white Sioux and a white she-demon—sent to test their cunning—had cost them seven braves and all the horses they'd stolen. One more scalp and at least one fine horse would save some of their honor.

Lampbertson raised his hands in a futile gesture of submission. A brave rushed forward and pulled the .36 Navy out of his holster.

"Hey there, chief." The gun hawk wrestled a nervous smile to his lips. "You got no quarrel with me. You understand me, Injun?"

"One thing will save you," War Moon answered in English, stoically raising his weapon from its low cant. "Red stone."

For a moment Lampbertson combed his brain to make sense of the cryptic message delivered in the savage's garbled English. Then seeing a last glimmer of chance, he remembered what Red Read had given him. He reached slowly into his pocket and fished out the smooth river rock. He held it out in a shaking palm.

"You mean like this?"

Ike Lampbertson had faced death before. A hangman's noose in St. Louis, an extremely angry father with a ten-gauge shotgun in some hick town near New Orleans. Yet his heart about burst with relief when he saw the jaw of the bronzed Indian go slack and his dark eyes swell in their sockets.

"It is just as the prophet foretold," War Moon gasped to his fellows in their language. A babble of amazement and awe ran through the ranks. The war chief took a step back and lowered his rifle. Ike's nervous smile tinged with arrogance.

"You boys savvy this, heh?" he asked, then laughed with contempt.

War Moon slapped his jaw back into place and tensed it. Lampbertson lost his arrogant leer, cleared his throat and waited.

The Kiowa-Apache chief looked back and found his most expendable man.

"Dark Cloud." The leader motioned the overweight, pockmarked warrior forward. "You will take this white man to Red Owl. The prophet has ordered this."

Eli walked Sonny back into the rocks, to find the young female captive dutifully starting a fire, nurturing it with twigs and blowing on it with a delicacy that he would have thought the hostiles had long ago beaten out of her. She looked up and smiled and Holten couldn't help but notice, among other things, the desperate longing in her eyes.

The girl rose in her tattered dress and curtsied. "We ain't been properly introduced, sir," she started. "My name is Louise Van Pelton and I'm beholden to you for saving my life from those savages."

Eli pulled his slouch hat from his head and smiled as best he could at the former captive.

"My name's Eli Holten, Miss Van Pelton, and I only wish we'd known you were a prisoner before we started after those Injuns. We would have caught up to them quicker."

Louise paled and a hand went to her mouth, the other to her crotch. Shock, the scout figured. Having twelve animals rape a girl her small size off and on over a couple of days while she remained constantly in fear for her life might cause a strange reaction when she got rescued.

"If I may call you Eli, sir, I would be honored if you'd call me Louise." The short, slender girl tugged on her lapel daintily and a cream-colored breast promptly slid out of a rip in her blouse. She seemed unaware of this. She smiled coyly as though flirting with a young man at a barn raising.

Her inviting innocence sent a warm shock through the

129

scout's groin, despite her tender years, and he slid his hat in front of him to shield his tightening pants. She's a child, he told himself sternly.

"Ma'am . . . Louise, if we mount up and head out like lightning, we could catch up with the people I came with. I imagine they're expecting to find us there anyway."

The girl blushed, a more angelic hue no cherub could possibly have in heaven. Holten's heartbeat raced and he again forced himself to consider her immature years.

"Of course, Eli, you know best. However, if we paused for a moment, perhaps I could make myself more presentable." With slim, pretty fingers, Louise stuffed her exposed breast back into her dress, only to have the other's nipple poke out of a different tear.

"I . . . I have needle and thread in my saddlebags, Louise," Eli croaked, his trousers straining with the building pressure within.

"I would be most grateful," Louise answered and Holten stared down into the limpid blue pools of her eyes. As he did, he couldn't help but wonder what she looked so hungry for.

Marshal Dorsey Wharton jiggled along on the back of his mule, headed for the XIT Ranch. First, though, he had to stop and get Tom Meyers out and joined up with Reagan to go into the Nations.

Meyer's simple soddy snuggled into the hard-packed ocher soil only a small distance from the border of the massive XIT Ranch. His cattle amounted to little more than a handful and his place looked rundown and unkempt. That didn't surprise the marshal.

Everyone knew that Meyers lived to work for the rangers. Dorsey couldn't think of any other man who hated Indians as much as the redheaded Meyers. His desire to exterminate them exceeded even that of the most rabid anti-native factions back East. And, boy, could Meyers track!

Though he never spoke about it, everyone figured Meyers must have been a scout for the Union Army at one time. His blue pants with the yellow stripe down the side, which he invariably wore when he went tracking, fairly well marked him. Probably a scout, all agreed, surely combat bred.

The marshal rode up and spotted a note hanging on the door to the soddy. Wharton slipped his glasses on as he pushed his mount out from under him and walked to the delapidated porch.

The note read simply: *Hav gon to tend my catel. Leav messag ef you need me. Tom Meyers.*

"Damned kid," Dorsey cursed, digging in his pockets for the pencil he always brought with him. "You can never find him when you need him."

The marshal located his pencil, licked its tip and started writing on the back of the paper with Tom's message. *Tom. Reagan's goin after Kiowa-Apaches in the territory. Needs you to track. Catch up with them on Ft. Sill Trail if you can.*

Wharton dated it, then signed his name.

"Damn lucky I can read an' write, Meyers," he grumbled, then started as he heard something.

A noise, some motion, came from the corral around the side.

"That you, Tom?" Wharton bellowed and started walking around the corner of the soddy.

As he cleared the edge of the building, the marshal walked headlong into an apparition, some hideous mirage that Dorsey couldn't explain. Wharton knew instantly what he faced wasn't right. Yet it seemed so familiar. He opened his mouth to say something, but sharp agony froze his words in his throat.

Red Owl pulled his lance free of the white man's fat

belly. He jerked Wharton's intestines, ripped and bloody, out with it. Even after the weapon broke free, Dorsey's guts continued to ooze out, as though they'd been under constraint, and now that the walls that held them together had been rent, they would spurt onto the dusty ground in front of Wharton until the pressure had been spent.

At last his throat opened and a shriek of pain and terror flashed to the heavens. The screaming marshal fell to his knees and tried to hold his steaming entrails in with his hands. Once the dam had broken, however, there seemed no way to stop it.

The prophet stepped around the sod-block building with his rifle to see if anyone had come with the marshal. The medicine man smiled grimly as he reassured himself Wharton had come alone.

The scrap of paper still hung in Wharton's fingers. Curious, Red Owl leaned down and jerked the blood-soaked fragment out of the dying white man's hand. Red Owl wiped the gore off and concentrated mightily to make out what Dorsey had written. Then he smiled as the message the marshal wrote became clear in his eyes.

Twelve

Eli prepared a noonday meal as he watched Louïse try to
repair her dress. First she worked on the torn skirt and
hem, carefully plying the needle back and forth through
the sturdy cotton material. Holten began to think she
didn't notice her luscious bounty slipping out of the
many tatters and rips in her blouse. Then she started
reaching up on occasion and shoving a creamy globe back
under the cloth.

The dress seemed too tight to begin with and, leaning
over to work on it, Louise's endowments spent more time
out than in. The effort she put into manipulating her
splendid facets had Eli hard pressed to keep his mind on
the beans, biscuits, and coffee he prepared. It became
obvious to him that the girl intended to take her dear
sweet time fixing the damage to her clothes. Her eyes
focused with concentration on the delicate work, her
pink tongue sticking out of a corner of her mouth. The
scout went to where he had tied up the horses. He
loosened the cinch on Sonny and fed both animals.

133

Finally, hoping to move the girl along, Eli returned to the fire.

"Would you like something to eat, Louise?"

"Oh, I'd dearly love that," the girl cooed through a smile. Then a pout came to her face. "I fear I have no utensils to eat with."

Holten had only his own set of eating tools and his stomach protested any acts of chivalry, like offering them to the girl. Then he thought of a solution.

"I'll be right back," he told the girl.

"All right. I'll keep working on my clothes."

Holten picked up his Winchester and headed west. Out ahead he saw the shock of Johnson Grass where Shorty had made his last stand. Nearby, Shorty's pony lay dead. Eli walked to its stiffening form as flies buzzed the flesh. With a few quick jerks, Holten had the saddle off. Shorty's bedroll came with it. In there, or in the saddlebags, Holten knew, the cowboy would have his eating kit.

Eli walked back with his prize, entering among the rocks with a quiet tread. He nearly had the roll opened when he came into the clearing. Instantly, his attention got rerouted.

Louise Van Pelton sat demurely on a rock, her dress draped over her lap, herself bare as the way nature made her, smiling up from her perch. The bedroll fell open in Eli's hands. Shorty's mess kit thudded into the sand.

"Oh!" the naked girl cried as she rose.

Louise looked like a tight-coiled spring, wrapped in ermine. Her flesh, firm and hard, shined like silver with her whiteness in the sun. Her breasts, freed from the tight dress, swung tautly, large and firm, with pointed pink nipples that seemed to swell with Eli's gaze. A full, bushy blond thatch offered the only cover for the crevice between her legs which seemed to be sweating in the noonday sun.

134

"You found something I can use!" Louise enthused and never implied she knew where they came from, or that she stood there naked.

It dawned on Eli about that time that little Louise Van Pelton would be a wonderful thing to make some loving with and that the girl wanted to with an urgency he rarely expected in one so young. Knowing that made the levelheaded scout feel regret. He could only anticipate what would obviously come next, and wonder at how he would react. The luscious morsel of a woman-child walked gracefully to where the kit had fallen, dragging her dress behind her, then bent down to gather the utensils.

When she rose, Eli saw the same hungry look in her eyes that he noticed when he first met her, only it seemed more intense and its meaning could be easily read. He cleared his throat and licked suddenly dry lips. He knew he had to busy himself feeding Louise, though that wouldn't give her what she *really* wanted.

In strained silence the pair returned to the fire. The girl hauled the blanket back as well. She sat on it and politely let Eli serve her a large helping of navy beans, a sourdough biscuit, and a tin of Arbuckle's coffee.

Eli appreciatively studied the alabaster vision eating on a dead man's blanket in front of him. He wondered how a girl who had surely had to suffer the indignity of multiple rape could want yet another man. Her every movement made her purpose clear. Perhaps she needed a white to prove to herself she still attracted the right kind of person. Perhaps, he thought grimly, something had snapped loose in her mind.

"How did you end up in the Kiowa-Apaches' hands?" he asked to make conversation.

Louise's face twisted into sadness with the question, then the girl told a sad story about losing her family in the Panhandle, never knowing her father, who'd died when she was very young, and her mother joining her father in the grave not long ago in Lubbock. A kindly family took her in as they headed north on a dream of their own. They had joined a wagon train and, Louise explained, that was where her troubles began.

"The other women never liked me," Louise sniffed out. "When the Injuns showed up, the old sows made the men give me to the savages to save the wagon train." She looked away and sighed sadly, feeling the martyr. To Holten, it somehow didn't ring true. Then Louise continued.

"I suppose one orphan's life for the entire train was a fair trade."

During this sad reminiscence, Louise's hands had crossed over her chest, as though to hold herself in her misery. Then she began to fondle her breasts. The beautiful young girl seemed quite adept at kneading her soft white pillows, absently working down to her bright, pink nipples which she played and teased until they stood erect. Her hands slid from her chest to her crotch. The scout noticed her blond pubic hair glistened with even greater moisture in the sun. All told, he felt sure there was something she had left out about conditions on that wagon train. Louise looked to Eli and smiled sadly.

"I'm forever grateful to you for saving me."

"My pleasure, Louise." Despite his determination not to let the young girl affect him, Holten's voice came out thick and husky, watching the gorgeous morsel of womanhood massaging herself, her breath growing wispy with her self-stimulation.

Languidly Louise removed her hands from between her legs, fell to all fours and, with the fluid motion of a cat, crawled to where Eli sat. Her hands exploded outward, with nimble-fingered experience, undoing Holten's britches with such speed that he had no chance to protest and could only marvel at the gifted youngster's talents.

The scout's rebelliously swelling staff sprang out and Louise cried with delight.

"My, Eli, you are blessed!"

Holten swallowed hard. He had to stop this. "H-how old are you, Louise?"

The girl frowned in concentration. "Goin' on fifteen, I think."

With that, the girl swallowed his love-lance in one prodigious gulp.

Gently, Eli reached out and took her by the shoulders. He tried to pull her away from his pulsating manhood. But the tugging of her lips, dexterous strokes of her tongue and powerful suction she applied sent shivers of delight through his lean frame. For a long moment his resolve faltered.

She's only fourteen, for God's sake, his mind rebuked him. He shoved with increased strength and extricated his glowing, tingingly wet penis from her mouth.

"Why?" Louise gasped, her favors having never been refused before. "Don't you want me?"

"Y-yes, I do, Louise. That's the trouble. Later on it would be welcome. Perhaps in a . . . a few years, when you've grown up," he finished lamely, his burning body giving ample physical evidence of the conflict between it and his conscience.

Louise's face crumpled. She threw her arms around Holten's shoulders, buried her face against his chest and began to sob. "B-b-but, I w-want y-you n-n-now!" she wailed.

Holten embraced her in a fatherly manner and, for a long time, he, too, wanted to cry.

*　　*　　*

War Moon and what few warriors survived the white Sioux's attack straggled into the Indian agent's station near Fort Sill. The Kiowa-Apaches had lost seven of their men. Five to Tall Bear, one to the boy who rode with him and one to the cowboys when the white men came up on the herd of stolen horses. Now only five warriors remained.

The clapboard cabins that spread out across the treeless hill had been laid out in orderly fashion. The main house, where the Indian agent and his wife lived and had his office, sat imposingly toward the top of a low knoll, with the storage facility to its right and the Quaker meeting house on the left.

Between the church and the main building, a corral for horses and some livestock held several handsome ponies. War Moon studied them with envy and wondered if, after they'd been resupplied by Leroy Barker with food and ammunition, they might steal some horses while at the white man's buildings. No, he rejected, the soldiers lived too close by, at the place called Fort Sill. Contempt mirrored in War Moon's eyes as he thought of the pitiful wretches who had taken the white man's road, whom they had seen on the way in.

The warriors had led their horses past fields of halfheartedly plowed ground that the reservation dwellers had furrowed in the red clay soil, to placate the agent. Only scraggly stalks of ill-tended grain showed for their efforts. The people had grown listless and sullen. The agent had failed in his attempts to pacify the Kiowa, Shawnee, and Cheyenne, no matter what the rosy reports he wrote back to the Bureau of Indian Affairs and the Society of Friends.

These free-roaming braves walked their horses past rows of tipis where these shamefaced, helpless Indians waited for their next ration of food and clothing from the BIA. Young boys came screaming out, leading the way for the war party, running ahead and announcing War Moon's arrival. He and his men passed the squalor with heavy hearts and a tinge of contempt. They came to the white man's barn, where cows stood ready for milking and meat cattle waited to be slaughtered. These places smelled of plenty, while the stench of starvation, sickness, and death hung over those who had traded their bows and rifles for blankets and handouts. At the war leader's direction, they made straight for the main building, where Mr. and Mrs. Jeremiah Turpin waited on the porch.

Turpin, dressed in the full black garb of the Quakers, with his wife behind and to his right, wearing the women's gray habit of their cult, came down the steps. Jeremiah's smile could have been on the Madonna's face when Jesus came into the world as he greeted the six scalp-toting warriors.

"Greetings to the Kiowa-Apaches," the agent said in polished Kiowa. "We greet you as friends and brothers to our home. I am Jeremiah Turpin, called White Peace Pipe by thy brother red men who live here with us. This is my woman, April."

Jeremiah used the Kiowa word for spring to designate his wife's name. The savages glanced stoically at each other. Although not spoken in their own language, they recognized the words well enouh and were pleased by them. They had been told the Indian agents here could be manipulated to one's needs. War Moon turned back to Turpin, thrust his chest out and grimaced.

"I am called War Moon, leader of these men. I have come searching for a white man named Leroy Barker," he announced in English.

The agent had to squeeze his face muscles to keep smiling.

"We have not seen friend Barker for many moons. If you seek him, I'm sure he is only delayed. Would it be unwise to ask why you wish to see this white man?"

"He told us to meet him here," War Moon answered, noting that obviously the agent didn't like Barker. "He said he had many things to trade with us."

Jeremiah, a round-faced, well-fed man, with bright cheeks and handsome white teeth, nodded. He well understood what they meant. An evil man, he thought. He would have to do all he could to keep these innocent children apart from Barker.

"Oh, I see. Friend War Moon, if friend Barker does not arrive soon, perhaps I could be of assistance. Here we are all brothers. Is there anything thee needs?"

War Moon blanched at the suggestion that Barker or Turpin might be his brothers, by blood or by choice. His reaction, however, proved too subtle for the agent to catch. Cryptically, the war chief spoke.

"Food and blankets, sugar and coffee."

War Moon listed everything his group needed, except ammunition. He'd been warned not to come right out and ask for that. Tensely he waited for the strange white man's response.

Jeremiah looked back at his wife and they smiled angelically at each other. "All these things the White Grandfather and the Society of Friends can give thee, if thee will give up thy warring ways and live in peace here on the reservation," the agent intoned like a minister speaking of the goodness of God. "Thee will not need the services of friend Barker."

The warriors considered this, stone faces turning to exchange knowing glances. War Moon crossed his arms over his chest and nodded sharply.

Several employees of the post, at Turpin's direction, began gathering the requested goods from the stores while Jeremiah and April, a thin, matronly woman with a wrinkled neck and horn-rimmed glasses, shaded by her plain, gray bonnet, smiled at their new prospects and at each other.

"Thee has been most generous with War Moon, husband," she whispered. "Dost thee knowest some secret that makes this opportune?"

"Only that the man these innocent children of nature seek is a scoundrel who barters out demon rum to the naive people we shepherd. Better that we give them everything they need, than he giving them what their weak natures might want."

Jeremiah walked to one corner of the cache building, made sure that no one saw him remove the key from his pocket, and opened a large wooden trunk. Inside, besides the revolvers and carbines the army had issued the reservation for defense and the establishment of an Indian police force, lay enough ammunition for a small war. The Quakers, of course, had no use for guns. So nothing had been done toward these goals. Their only accomplishment had been to bring the good news of the Bible to the natives and obtain the money from the government to press forward with their social experiment through the BIA at "pacifying and Christianizing" the many tribes relocated into the Indian territory. Though the agent and his employees used no firearms, they constantly needed more ammunition, and the army, ordered by the BIA through the War Department, kept restocking it.

April saw her spouse throw cartons of several different kinds of ammo into a large flour sack.

"Husband, dear, dost thee think these new friends need that much ammunition for hunting game?" she asked sharply when he'd returned to the front of the store with the bag.

"No, dear wife. Yet, did thee not see the six horses with blankets and bridles, but no riders? Did thee not see the fresh scalps which friend War Moon has on his lance? Our red brothers have been attacked." Jeremiah nodded

141

vigorous assurance at the look of outraged disbelief on his wife's face.

"Who?" she asked.

"Soldiers or white bandits, surely, or sinful, greedy drovers hauling cattle up the Chisholm Trail to the dens of iniquity in Kansas. They will need this to protect themselves from the evil white men of this earth until they have Him protecting them, as we are protected."

April considered this a moment. "Are thee sure thee have the right calibers, husband?" she asked sweetly.

Jeremiah handed the war chief the sack as the agency's employees loaded the other goods on the riderless horses, while the now mounted warriors sat impassively on their ponies. War Moon opened the bag to discover his booty and, despite his warrior's training, his eyes glowed with excitement.

"May I offer a small piece of advice along with this gift of friendship, friend War Moon?" Jeremiah inquired. "Avoid white men like Leroy Barker. They are evil and full of vile goals. They will sell thee diabolical goods, like . . . well, perhaps it is wiser not to intrigue thee with their names. Leroy Barker does not love thee like we here at the reservation. Stay away from him."

War Moon quickly calculated about two hundred rounds of ammunition in the gunnysack. He looked up at the agent, realizing only toward the end of the little speech that Turpin spoke to him. The chief could only nod at Jeremiah. Then, fearing the Indian agent might want something more tangible in return, War Moon turned his pony and dug his heels into its bare flanks, only waving back at the reservation residents once out of range.

With racuous laughter the six Indians reined their mounts in as they crested a hill and set about measuring their gifts.

"The Quakers must hate the white people as much as

us," Red Pony cried as War Moon handed out the ammunition.

"They are great allies and we must treat them well," War Moon declared. "Perhaps it is the sickness which robs a man of his reason, for they, too, are white. If that is so, we will protect them and shelter them, for it makes them holy. If not, then they will be the last white people we kill in this war."

"It is the medicine of Red Owl," Cold Wind exclaimed. "Once we proved our cunning by getting rid of Little Yellow Bush, we could use his medicine more completely."

The others nodded agreement and shared new wonderment at the prophet.

"Don't be angry at me," Louise pleaded when the sobbing subsided. "Please. It's . . . only that I haven't had a man for the longest time. Not since . . . why, not since this morning when you boys came over that ridge and scared the Indians away."

Holten shook his head in dismay. Then he felt a jolt of electrified joy as Louise wrapped her small, warm fingers around the thick shaft of his rigid manhood. Slowly she began to stroke the loose skin, teasing him with this stimulation of the greater gift she offered.

"Louise . . . stop that. We can't . . . I mean, your age. You are so young."

Louise only tightened her grip and increased the speed of her surging hand. "Back home in West Virginia, most girls my age are married and have a baby or two. I . . . I'm not so little," she declared with indignation. "I can take every inch you've got. And . . . oh, I love it so."

Holten could only groan.

Louise felt the pulse of Holten's blood in the silken rod she played with, and her own heart raced in tune. She

143

bent down and covered the dark red tip with her full, sweet lips and began to take him in a bit at a time.

"No! Stop it Louise. Stop or . . . damnit . . . I . . . I'll . . ."

Under the unearthly influence of Louise's fervid desire, Holten's defenses crumbled one at a time. She had nearly consumed all of him, one hand gently squeezing his potent sack, when the pounding of hoofs, drawing rapidly near, galvanized both of them into hurried action.

"Who . . . who could it be?" Louise inquired with a trembling voice after disengaging herself from his vibrating prong.

"I don't know. Could be War Moon coming back."

"Oh!"

"You had better get dressed. There, behind that rock."

Five minutes later, Les Thacker trotted into the narrow opening to the clearing, leading an extra pony behind his paint. "What the hell are you doing, Holten?" he cried. "You stop for a siesta in the middle of the day?"

"Only tidying up after the Kiowa-Apaches. Good to see you, Les. We have ourselves a guest," Holten told him as Louise, fully dressed, came from hiding behind a boulder.

Thacker's jaw dropped at the sight of the delightful girl. Then a knowing glint came to his eyes. Holten, behind Louise, slowly shook his head in negation.

"She's the one the Kiowa-Apaches had prisoner. Louise Van Pelton, this is Ranger Les Thacker."

After the introductions, Eli feared that Louise would try her wiles on the young Texan, so he moved to prevent it. "We've some bodies to bury," he told Thacker. "Booger and that boy, Shorty. While we do that, Louise can start grub. Too late to ride out tonight."

"Too bad about Shorty. I sorta liked the kid. A lot like me at his age."

While Louise started preparing the night's meal, Eli

and Les went to bury the two boys who had died in the attack.

"Would've gotten back to you sooner, but Zeke and his drovers were bound and determined to get back to the herd."

"What the hell are we going to do with the girl?" Eli asked, deciding it prudent to not comment on Louise's peculiarities. "I was counting on Newman to take her to Wichita."

"No problem," Les replied as he patted down the dirt on Shorty Duessen. "We'll drop her off at Fort Sill. Or maybe the Indian agent there will take her in. Understand they're good Christian folk."

Eli stared down at the final resting place of the young drag rider. He pulled his hat off long enough to pay the brave boy a moment's respect. What had Dirty Dave said when the swing man suggested the boy would be moving up next year? Only if he lived out this one, Dave had said. Shorty hadn't made it.

Louise slept soundly through the whole night. Eli, though, turned and twisted on his blanket. His groin ached from unfulfillment yet he sought to rebuild his resolve not to dally with the energetic Louise. Despite his best intentions, he thought of her as she had been on that long afternoon and received only a throbbing erection as his reward.

The three set out shortly after sunrise, Louise apparently recovered for the moment. Holten put his worries behind him.

He would never have done so had he fully realized the danger of a walking volcano like Louise Van Pelton.

Thirteen

The Kiowa-Apache rider tore recklessly up the wagon trail, sparing neither himself nor his mount. The pony he rode lathered furiously. Leroy Barker, handing out fresh new Winchester Model '73 repeaters, looked up to see the small figure approaching. He ceased his dealings for gold watches and mementos taken off murdered settlers and cowboys to observe.

The young boy leaped from his chest-heaving animal and ran to War Moon, who recognized the messenger as the brother of Cold Wind. Their greetings were brief, almost perfunctory.

"Red Owl sent me," the youth blurted out. "He said to find you as quickly as I could."

"What does Red Owl want me to know?" War Moon demanded.

"Four hands of Texas Rangers are coming at you, led by the ranger chief, Reagan."

Scowling contemplation lined War Moon's face a moment as he visualized his five men facing a vastly

superior force of bloodthirsty rangers. In past encounters he had found the white warriors unnaturally
talented with their rifles. Yet, since they had rid
themselves of Little Yellow Bush, their hunger for
adventure seemed to be coming back. A slow smile
replaced his frown.

"What does Red Owl wish me to do with them?"

The boy paused to catch his breath and gather his
thoughts. "He wishes you to keep the ranger chief out of
Texas. To lead them away with small battles so that they
think all of our men fight with you."

War Moon straightened and looked to the south, as
though striving to see the Texans coming his way. Again
his brow furrowed.

"How can six of us fight so many and hope to keep
them busy for very long?" Cold Wind asked him, giving
voice to the leader's thoughts.

"I have a plan," War Moon answered. He turned again
to the messenger. "Take a fresh horse and ride quickly
back to Red Owl. Tell him that we found the white man
with the red rock and he is being taken to the prophet.
Tell him we shall do as he asked, but we need more men.
With them we will confuse the rangers and in the end
bring many warriors to join him."

Eli, Thacker, and Louise rode west and south now,
heading for Fort Still. Holten's thoughts were filled with
visions of the luscious Miss Van Pelton, while Les talked
of the country in the Panhandle. The ranger sniffed at
the air and sighed with contentment.

"Smell that good air? Do you smell it? It's full of the
scent of yellow roses. It's boiling with life! I tell you it's
the best air in all the world. The sweet air of Texas."

Holten snorted derisively, then stiffened. "Riders

148

coming," he announced, his head bowed slightly forward and his eyes staring sightlessly at the ground.

Thacker drew up his horse, listened for a moment, then a incredulous expression crinkled his face. "What'er you talking about, Eli?" he accused. "I can believe you could spot the animals with riders in a herd of horses and luck told you one horse carried a woman, but I'll be damned if you can tell if there's riders coming when there ain't no sound."

"There's plenty of sound," Holten countered, hesitated, then pulled his Winchester from its scabbard. He looked around, then turned Sonny toward a clump of scrub oak that offered some cover.

"You can't be serious," Thacker taunted.

"Louise, come on, get off the road." Holten pointed into the thicket.

"I can't believe this." Les stood in his stirrups. "How long you gonna stay in there, boy?"

"As long as it takes to identify those riders," Holten answered. "I figure you have about five minutes to find some cover."

The Texan laughed for a long time and pointed at the two people wandering off into the little oak trees. Abruptly he ceased his guffaws and listened for a moment. His eyes darted southward, then he tightened his jaw.

"Damn. I'll be damned."

"There's a spot right over here for you," Eli offered.

The ranger didn't hesitate. He urged his horse toward the hiding place as the rumble of horses moving at a steady gate broke the natural sounds of the bright spring day.

Even before the ranger settled into the spot next to Holten, a neat row of single-file riders started over a ridge no more than a few hundred yards away. Almost immediately Thacker stretched upward in his saddle.

"Hell, Eli, that's Captain Reagan."

The range foreman of the XIT Ranch, Eddie Quaid, rushed into the rambling adobe building and looked both ways before pulling off his hat. He loped past Mexican servants and rugged furniture and ran to a door in the far wall of the living room.

He hesitated there, then, getting up his courage, he walked on in.

"Hot shit on a skillet! What do you think you're doin' punchin' into my goddamned office like that?" a stout, tough-looking man behind the polished walnut desk cried out from his leather-bound chair.

"Sorry to bother you, Mr. Goodnight," Quaid answered. "It's an emergency. Some Kiowa-Apaches are raiding in the western end of the ranch."

"Shit!" Charlie Goodnight snarled through the drooping strands of his brown handlebar mustache. "You best get every goddamned hand together, send someone for the rangers and get all the fucking supplies you need for the ball-busting trail from the stores. Damnnit all! We got peace with the Comanches, scared crap outta the Kiowa and now we have these sonsofbitches comin' in here from New Mexico to bite our balls. Don't stand there, get a move on!"

Goodnight launched from his chair, tore a thick corduroy jacket from a peg and picked up a shiny one of a kind Winchester off the gun rack.

"Where'n hell is Oliver Loving?"

"W-well," Quaid stammered. "You had him up drinking and talking until about three hours ago. He might be sleeping."

"What a crock of shit," Goodnight responded. "I couldn't tell you how many times that hollow-legged

150

bullshitter has drunk me under the table."

"I'll go get him," Eddie volunteered as he darted for the door.

"Tell the old fart that we got some goddamned Injuns to kill," Goodnight yelled out. "That should perk him up."

Reagan peered at the three mounted figures ambling out of the scrub oak. He smiled with recognition and spoke in a gravelly rumble.

"I'd gotten a little worried about you two, and here I find you in the company of a beautiful lady."

Louise blushed demurely and started building up a sudden burst of youthful lustiness. Beside her, Holten paled slightly, aware now of the girl's interest in all these men.

"'Mornin', Cap'n," Les greeted. "I'd like to introduce you to Eli Holten, the best tracker and scout in all of Texas, an' that means the world."

"Well, Holten," Reagan ground out. "Sounds to me like you've received the best compliment a Texan can give."

"We were headed toward Fort Sill to drop the young lady off," Eli offered and felt like he'd met an old friend.

The smile on the captain's face, the relaxed way he moved and handled himself told the experienced tracker and judger of men that this Texas Ranger would be everything General Corrington said he'd be. Holten felt reassured. Here was a man, regardless of age, who could do the job. The rangers were tough, independent, yet Holten sensed they would follow this Captain Reagan readily. The captain's words interrupted the scout's evaluation.

"Sounds like we're all in luck," Reagan observed. "We got wind from a couple of local Indians that they spotted

Kiowa-Apaches up this way. We were headed for the trail. But since we're hunting Red Owl's people, we took the hint and did some cross tracking.''

"Find anything?" Eli asked.

"No, not yet. We couldn't get ahold of Tom. Tom Meyers is the best scout we have and he's a volunteer. Now we might have a chance of pinning the hostiles down.''

"Why would they be heading for Fort Sill with all those soldiers?" Holten inquired, genuinely puzzled.

"It's not the fort they might go to, it's the Indian agent's place," Reagan explained. "Sometimes if they get whupped, or they're looking for a free meal, they go there.''

"Well, they got whupped, cap'n," Wild Man Thacker bragged. "Eli an' me must have killed twenty of 'em between us.''

"There were only twelve to begin with, Les," Holten reminded him. He went on to explain the circumstances of the fight they had with War Moon's band and how they had gained the company of the young lady.

"I see," Reagan ground out softly, suspecting something had been left out. "We might as well go to the reservation, then. We'll leave Miss Van Pelton in the hands of the agent.''

The twenty rangers and the three new members of the group turned west. Before a mile had passed, though, Eli once again bowed his head.

"A lot of riders coming," Eli said almost to himself. "And I'll lay odds it's an army patrol.''

"Oh, now, Holten, you're pullin' m'leg," Thacker blustered. "I can believe your ears are better than mine and I'll buy you might hear some more riders coming, but I'll be damned if you can tell who they are from the sound of it.''

Eli didn't answer. He hadn't been listening to Wild

152

Man. He cocked his ear and concentrated a moment longer, then smiled and nodded his head.

"Sure enough. A company of cavalry. They're traveling in formation. I've heard the way that sounds often enough to know it. I even think I hear a sergeant bellowing."

"Which way?" Reagan asked.

"From the west, headed toward us. Give them a minute to come over that hill there."

"Maybe we'd best not be seen here," one of the rangers commented from behind. "No doubt about it, we're out of our jurisdiction."

"If they're looking for bandits or Indians, they got scouts out that'll spot our trail. If they haven't made contact already," Eli observed. "If we try to run off, they'll follow us. Best to meet some problems straight on."

A strident shout came from the west, a voice most of the men recognized as the leather lungs of a top noncom. Over a slight roll in the prairie the gold tip of a guidon appeared.

"In fact," Captain Reagan announced, "it's probably best we go meet this one."

The large contingent of rangers moved out, headed west, and crested the hill in front of them. From there the two bodies of white men could see each other. The rangers reined in as the commander of the cavalry unit raised his hand, and the First Sergeant bellowed, "Company . . . *halt!*"

"Eli," Reagan started, "why don't you ride out with me. Thacker, you, too."

The rangers and the scout trotted forward, while the army officer, accompanied by a sergeant and the guidon bearer, rode to meet the civilian-clothed men halfway. Horses nickered and bits jingled in the quiet and in the distance a meadowlark trilled.

153

"Good morning, lieutenant," the ranger captain greeted.

"Good day to you, sir," the officer answered. Then he recognized the Twelfth Cavalry scout.

"Holten!" he shouted exuberantly.

"Lieutenant Taylor," Eli answered.

"Hi, there, lieutenant," Thacker chimed in. "How's your wife?"

"Somehow this isn't like I pictured it," Reagan remarked to no one in particular.

"We met on the train to Wichita," Holten explained with a smile. He turned back to the army officer. "This here's Capt. Duke Reagan, Company D, Ranger Frontier Battalion."

"You know you're out of your jurisdiction," Taylor rebuked good-naturedly.

"Guilty as charged," Reagan acknowledged cheerfully. "We heard that Kiowa-Apaches have been raiding on the trail, and for the last couple of months, we've been getting hit pretty bad by them. They got a new prophet, and all I can say is, he has powerful medicine on his side."

"Look, captain," Taylor started. "I'm sympathetic to your problem, but my orders aren't. It isn't what the army wants, it's what the Indian agents demand that puts us on opposite sides. Those crazy Quakers practically run this territory, with all the blessings you could want. At least around here. According to Turpin—that's the agent—the army's the problem, not the hostiles. Fort Sill heard about the attacks on the Chisholm Trail even before I got there, but we caught so much lecturing from the agent that it took us this long to get permission to go out and check."

"That's preposterous!" Reagan thundered.

"I know it is. But there's a lot of sympathy being generated back East about the plight of the poor Indians.

'Lo, the noble savage' has replaced earlier thinking. With all the corruption in the Grant administration, the BIA is under fire. They're sensitive to public whim. At the core of it are the Quakers. Punitive expeditions are frowned on. A third of the reservations are run by the Society of Friends right now. *They* call the tune."

"Well, fuck Mr. Lo and all his red brothers. These Kiowa-Apaches are killing Texans and I intend to make 'em pay for it."

Young Taylor shrugged and sighed regretfully. "That's why I'm obliged to ask you to leave the territory. I'm even supposed to escort you out."

"Probably for the best for you, lieutenant, that we're joining forces," Eli injected. "We ran into the raiders and we think they're headed for Turpin's place."

Taylor thought a moment. "We could escort you out by way of the reservation, couldn't we?"

The contingent of rangers and soldiers stopped more than a mile from the Indian agent's headquarters. There, it had been agreed, they would part company.

"I've never met the Indian agent," Taylor explained. "But from what I've been told, if Turpin sees this many armed white people, he'll scream all the way back to Washington. The word around the fort is that he's more extreme than his fellow Quakers. Most of them own a rifle or two for hunting. It's war they oppose. But this Turpin. He has some queer notion that guns were made for the exclusive use of the Indians and that all white men are evil—himself and his wife exempted, of course."

"Crazy," Reagan summed up in a word.

While the rangers bided their time, the company of cavalry rode on. They walked their horses into the reservation compound, along with Louise Van Pelton, Thacker, and Holten. News of their approach had preceeded them.

Jeremiah Turpin came out of the barn where, in his self-enforced humility, he'd been feeding the animals. He scowled at the large number of soldiers. Realizing how ungodly his anger might appear, he forced a smile to his face.

"Good day to thee, lieutenant," he greeted Taylor. "A beautiful morning, is it not?"

"How do you do, sir," the officer stated, tipping his hat to the Indian agent. "I'm Lieutenant Taylor. I've recently been assigned to Fort Sill. I was out looking for some Kiowa-Apaches who have been raiding on the Chisholm Trail—"

"Who art these other men thee hast brought?" Turpin demanded, pointing rudely at the civilians.

"This here's Eli Holten, scout for the army. He found this young lady, taken captive by the Kiowa-Apaches we're looking for. And these other two are Texas Rangers who are looking for the same Indians."

"Thee art out of thy jurisdiction and trespassing, for the Indian territory is not a part of Texas." Turpin came close to snarling and his hatred could be seen in his flat, watery blue eyes.

"And that's why we're escorting them out of here," Taylor assured the agent. "We were wondering if you've seen any hostiles on the warpath. About six of them, near as I can tell."

A tall, lean woman, all in gray, stepped up next to Turpin.

"Allow me to introduce my wife, lieutenant," Turpin went on, seemingly oblivious to the true nature of the conversation. "This is April. April, this is Lieutenant Taylor from Fort Sill. These other *gentlemen* are for the most part unwelcome invaders of Indian territory."

Everyone tipped their hats to the lady, then Taylor forced a smile.

"Well, Mr. Turpin?"

"Humm?"

"Have you seen any Kiowa-Apaches on the warpath?"

"Oh, no, certainly not. All our children here are full of the Holy Spirit and worship peace."

"I'm talking about hostiles, Mr. Turpin. They live on no reservation and follow no rules. The only spirit they're full of is firewater and gunpowder."

Turpin effected to ignore him.

An old Cheyenne, bent with age, though his eyes shined sharply, had stepped forward and spoke in English. "I am Running Antelope. I saw some Kiowa-Apaches painted for war to the east yesterday," he wheezed out. "I was fishing and they rode right past me. Six of them. War Moon led them. I know him from the before times. I recognized Cold Wind and Red Pony, too. I'm a Cheyenne," he added as if to assure the whites he told the truth.

"Perhaps they removed their paint and came in peacefully, Mr. Turpin," Taylor pressed. "Did you by chance give supplies to War Moon and his men?"

Jeremiah reinforced his rigid smile. "I have not seen that child of God for some time now."

"Now hold on d'here, Mistah Turpin."

An astonishingly large, broad-shouldered Negro, a pot belly stretching at his infantry uniform, stepped from the shadows of the storage room. He straightened up and gave a smart salute to the lieutenant.

"Sergeant Loper, suh, Twenty-fifth Infantry, A Company. I came over on my leave to see my woman, she wo'k here an' I sees these Injuns. Kiowa-Apaches, sure as I'm black as a kettle. They was talkin' wif de Turpins, an' de agent, he done give 'em supplies an' mebbe some ammo in a white flour sack."

Mrs. Turpin smiled euphorically at the black man, willing him to fall in line. "You must be mistaken, Jim."

"Naw, ma'am. I seen what I seen."

Eli had let his horse wander over to a corner of the compound near the warehouse. He stared at the ground for a moment, then turned back to the lieutenant and Captain Reagan.

"Those folks are lying," Holten whispered to the two men. "I recognized a hoof print over near the storage door. It has a prominant Y-shaped crack that I spotted on the Chisholm Trail when we were tracking the Kiowa-Apaches."

Reagan sighed with disgust. "You're protecting murderers, you know that?"

"Lieutenant," Turpin said coldly, "tell your prisoner that I do not speak to criminals such as himself. Sinners like him are not content to steal the land given to the Plains tribes until the sun doesn't shine and the water doesn't run. They have to violate treaties protecting what little the poor innocents have left."

"What else can you tell us, Sergeant?" Taylor asked, ignoring the sermon.

"Dats pretty much all I saw," Jim Loper responded. "I figured dose red men like as kill me an' have a woolly brush fo' dere *coup* sticks iffin I gets too nosey."

"Did you see anything else, Running Antelope?" Reagan inquired of the old Indian.

"Friend Cheyenne," Turpin cut in. "Thee hast lied against thy brother red men. If thee persists, the White Grandfather in Washington and the Society of Friends will not feed thee any more. Nor any of thy family."

The old man bristled, then his gaze dropped to the ground and he clamped his mouth shut. He looked up with regret at the mounted white men, then swung around and strode imperiously off.

"What the hell is your problem, Turpin?" Taylor burst out. "Are you some kind of renegade to turn your back on your own kind to side with those murderers?"

158

"This outburst will not go unreported, lieutenant," Turpin snapped icily.

"I'm sure it won't. As a matter of fact, I'll file a report on it myself. Harboring criminals and obstructing justice are crimes I'm sure the army and the Interior Department will want to know of."

For a long moment, the young officer and the fanatic moralist locked their eyes in a contest of wills. To break the tension, Holten spoke up.

"We have this young lady." Eli pointed to his charge. "We'd like to leave her here."

"We will be glad to tend to her needs, friend Holten," April replied. "Come, child, we will get thee a bath and fresh clothes."

"You're going to be all right here, Louise," the scout assured the girl.

Louise didn't respond. She stared down at the many rows of tipis nearby and noted all the strapping young men and noble old grandfathers around them. She felt certain she would be happy here.

Fourteen

Goodnight and Loving led the way, Lieutenant Wilder-spin of the rangers hauling his unit of men behind. A swirling army of ranch hands followed them. Tom Meyers came riding back from the west, his hat flopping in the wind.

"This way!" he cried.

Up on the high-grass plains that stretched away from the Palo Duro's deep, vari-colored gorge, the contingent of rangers and civilians rode across a treeless expanse of lush, waving green. Bald splotches of red-brown earth provided the only relief from the monotonous sameness. At a lonely camp out near the edge of Canyon county, although nowhere near the end of the XIT Ranch, the white men came upon the swollen, scalped remains of three XIT range riders.

"They was lookin' for stray newborns, Mr. Good-night," Eddie Quaid explained.

"What a crock of shit," Goodnight answered. "I'm gonna take that boy-buggerin' Red Owl, tear his balls off, jam 'em down his throat and watch him choke to death.''

"I'm with you, Mr. Goodnight," Tom Meyers chimed in.

"Then let's go," Loving, a tall, lean man with a neatly cropped mustache urged.

"There's about six or seven riders headed for the New Mexico line," Meyers stated as he heeled his horse and took off to scout ahead.

Gradually the land turned more arid, cactus replaced buffalo grass and gritty sand the thick, black loam of well-sodded prairie. After less than an hour, Goodnight pulled his horse up to Wilderspin. He leaned in the saddle and shouted to the ranger officer.

"Me an' my boys are headin' back, Lieutenant."

"Why?" Wilderspin asked after a moment's shocked silence. "Tom'll get their scent and we'll catch up with them in no time."

"I don't want to go any damn further without Captain Reagan."

"The captain is far, far away, Mr. Goodnight—" The ranger pulled his argument short, smiled grimly and nodded. "You know what's best for you, Charlie. Me an' my rangers'll stay after them."

"You're a fucking good man, Wilderspin," Goodnight complimented sparingly.

The ranch hands reluctantly turned around and followed their boss. Once out of sight of the rangers, Loving reined up and brought the twenty cowboys to a halt.

"What the hell's going on, Charlie?" he demanded.

"I think those thrice-damned savage sonsofbitches are doubling back to raid the ranch house, Oliver."

Loving's eyes grew wide. "How can you be so sure?"

"We've swung damn near due north over the last half hour. They ain't headed for sanctuary in fucking New

162

Mexico. Besides, that bastard Red Owl isn't the only one with powerful medicine, that's how." He gave his longtime partner a slow wink. "Let's move, damnit!"

Running Antelope heeled the agency mule he rode with all the strength he could muster. He intercepted the rangers and troopers an hour after their departure from the reservation.

"Greetings, Grandfather," Eli said in passable Cheyenne.

The old man beamed and replied in the same tongue. "I have come to tell you all I know. I am Cheyenne and once rode with the Dog Soldier Society. The Kiowa-Apache are my enemy."

"Let us speak in English, Grandfather, so that the others may know what we say."

Running Antelope nodded agreement. "War Moon is gathering all the hot young men of the tribes. Not the people of the Five Civilized Nations, but the new ones sent here by the whites. He urges them to follow the red one, the man they call Red Owl, who is ripe with much power."

"Is there really a Red Owl, then?" Reagan asked.

"I do not think his true name is Red Owl," Running Antelope wheezed out. "I do not know his real name, and War Moon is not saying."

"Why do they call him Red Owl?" Holten pressed.

"I do not know, but he possesses great and powerful medicine."

"And he's calling together all the hot heads in a general uprising?" Taylor concluded, concerned for the army's role in this event.

"Yes. All the young ones who feel confined. It is a bad thing." The old man straightened and added, "I have risked everything to tell you this. I am Cheyenne."

"Thank you, Grandfather," Taylor answered. Holten suppressed a smile of approval. Young Taylor was learning fast. The officer turned to the ranger captain.

"Well, Reagan, it looks like you're going to have to escort yourself out of here. I have to get back to Fort Sill and report this."

"A general uprising is going to get a lot of people killed," Reagan sighed.

"It's strange," Taylor remarked to no one in particular. "Before the Quakers and their great experiment, the Five Civilized Tribes had everything figured for themselves. They had laws and ways of enforcing them. Along comes the Society of Friends—with the backing of the Interior Department—and the first thing they try to do is shut down the Cherokee Light Horse, the Indians' means of keeping the peace. The new crop of agents say it is because the Cherokee are pagan and remind the army that they fought for the Confederacy. Then they hogtie the army's hands because, they tell Washington, we are too violent.

"As a result, the Nations have become a haven for all sorts of riffraff. Not just hostiles who ride in here all peaceful like to rest up between raids in Kansas and Texas, but white outlaws who have no law to fear except the federal marshals from Fort Smith and Judge Parker's gallows. All the while, this organized group of Indian agents keep agitating to see that the army has to stay out of it. The truth of the matter is the people who are getting protected by the Quakers are the renegades, hostiles, and criminals, while the Indians who are only trying to live in peace are being punished."

"That's a mighty long speech for you, Lieutenant," Holten observed.

"And I mean every word of it. I tell you, Eli, these

Quakers could bring about the destruction of all of us."

War Moon stood among the many whooping warriors, handing out crocks full of potent drink that burned the men's tongues and made them insane. He took a long pull from one such container and raised it above his head.

"Hear me, brothers. Though you are Cheyenne or Kiowa or Osage, we are all as one!" War Moon boomed over the pandemonium. "The Red Owl will bring us glory and many *coups*. He will bring back the buffalo even as we rid the earth of the white-eyes. They took your land and pushed you out to this wasteland. We will take it back!"

The Kiowa-Apache war leader yelled this mostly in English, the only common language to the majority of the mixed young warriors. They reacted with louder cheers and a variety of war whoops while the English speakers translated the words to those of their tribe who did not understand.

"How many of you are with us?"

The entire band shouted out their loud support.

War Moon led them to where Leroy Barker waited beside a buckboard stacked high with long crates of rifles.

"These are the gifts of the Red Owl to those who would follow him!" War Moon bellowed. "Those who have brothers and cousins in other camps, go now and gather them up and tell them this. For every white man you kill, a buffalo bull will appear on the plains. For every white woman you kill, ten cows will join that bull. This is what Red Owl has prophesied!"

For the first time, Leroy Barker began to feel a real chill of unease. Whipped up by such powerful words, drunk on rot-gut and armed to the teeth, it wouldn't take these savages long to realize *he* was the closest white man around to bring them a shaggy new buff bull. Leroy's eyes shifted from one knot of warriors to the next, weighing their temperament, and his hand unconsciously strayed in the direction of the Smith and Wesson revolver jammed in his waistband.

The horde of cowboys careened into the Palo Duro Canyon headquarters of the XIT Ranch. They ran their horses into the corral and swung off their mounts under a steady shower of lead and arrows. Quickly they scurried for cover.

At least fifty Kiowa-Apaches were shooting hell out of the place.

Leaping from one piece of cover to the next, the ranch hands, led by their boss, inched toward the ranch house. They returned fire as they went, urged on by a continuous stream of blue profanity from Charlie Goodnight.

"We didn't get here none too soon," Oliver Loving cried out.

"Just in time to get fucking massacred!" Goodnight observed.

Tom Meyers peered over the ridge with Wilderspin right behind him. They hadn't seen any tracks for five miles and the lieutenant looked impatient.

"We can't turn back just like that," the scout burst out.

"If we turn around right now we could get to the XIT headquarters tomorrow afternoon at the latest," Wilderspin answered calmly. "We've lost the trail and old Goodnight was adamant about going back. The way I figure it, he had a good reason."

Fury boiled scarlet in Meyers's face. "I wish the hell I'd been here when he deserted," the scout spat.

"Doesn't think much of his men if he let them get killed that way and won't get even for it.."

Wilderspin stroked his lantern jaw and fixed his pale, gray eyes on the excited younger man. "Face it, Tom, we ain't found shit. Even a greenhorn could figure out that the trail we've been on has swung in a circle. Goodnight is as brave as he is foulmouthed, Tom. You know that. Whatever he went back for, I figure it must have been important to him. Since this trail has gone cold, I think we ought to swing that way and find out if this all adds up."

"I'll tell you what," Meyers replied. "I'll go back and see what's going on. I can get there much quicker than the whole detachment. I'll find out and ride back. I'll stop long enough to change horses and get a bite to eat. Press on and keep a lookout for campfire smoke. Those Injuns don't expect us to be coming."

"I don't see as how we're gonna find any Indians out here." Wilderspin sighed and looked westward. "All right, Tom, we'll go a little further and do some cross tracking. We'll stay out here for the night, but you damn well hurry."

"I'll be back before you know it," Meyers flung over his shoulder as he heeled his horse and shot off toward the Palo Duro.

The tidy Cherokee village huddled into a crook of pine, far enough away from the nearby creek to avoid any water from spring flooding. Childen played around the stout wooden houses, and the few men present tended to their crops and livestock. The horses and valuables, food and weapons, impressed on War Moon that these "civilized" Indians enjoyed a great deal of wealth and comfort unknown to his own wild band.

He scooted further into the pines and turned to the

young Comanche warrior who had led them there.

"You are sure the Cherokee Light Horse is nowhere near?"

"They are far to the east by the white man's cattle trail." His lips curled with contempt. "The new agents have robbed them of their courage. They only enforce the white man's law and can not protect their own people. It will take them days to hear about this and by that time we will be in Texas with Red Owl."

The war leader nodded, then a smile ached at his stone face. He wanted to kill white men. The deaths of these Cherokee, though, would help him in his goal. Besides, the Cherokee were hardly more than whites. They wore the clothes, rode in wagons and tended the soil like the whites. He had heard they also had knowledge of how to put the marks on paper that others could understand. Their skins might be still of the real People, but in their hearts they had become white. War Moon raised his arm in a signal.

The large body of raiders swept down into the town from above, catching the residents off guard. They only had time to fire a few shots before being plowed down. War Moon led with his lance and howled gloriously as he caught a young boy in the chest.

With the power of his pony pushing him on, the long staff dug deeply into the child's breast. Blood burst from the Cherokee's mouth as the steel-tipped weapon ravaged his small lungs. The lance snapped in two close to the attacking warrior's hands as the mortally wounded youngster fell. War Moon pulled his new Winchester and rapidly fired and rechambered rounds as the war party rode through the streets.

The blood-drunk raiders jumped from their horses, beginning the ritual practice of rape and mutilation as they stripped the houses of any goods worth stealing. Here and there, a brave sliced the throats of the screaming women and children after they had been raped and sodomized.

A dust cloud rose to cover the scene and flames began to flicker from the wooden houses. The air grew rank with the odors of blood and death. Sated, the raiders rode out again, intoxicated with dreams of glory and ample portions of rot-gut whiskey left over from the earlier war dance.

Eli arrived at a vantage point shortly before the mixed band of hostiles had finished their gruesome sack of the Cherokee village. He watched helplessly from across the creek as the carnage went on. Holten boiled with anger as the attackers butchered the shrieking women and children in a fit of bloodlust. Grim-faced, he stayed to the last, then headed back to where he'd left the rangers.

The sun faded quickly in the west as Holten entered the ranger's night camp. Cook fires had been banked low and the Texas lawmen sat about eating the evening meal. The aroma of bacon, beans, and cornbread filled the air and cleansed the stench of death from the scout's nostrils.

"I found them," Holten announced coldly to Reagan. The leathery skin of the ranger captain's face undulated into a smile, then slid back, grimly, to match the icy visage of his scout.

"We in any kind of hurry?" he asked.

"No. They massacred a Cherokee village and loaded up on plenty loot and liquor they got from somewhere. They're in no hurry. We can catch up to them anytime now. But . . . it's not just Kiowa-Apaches anymore. There's Comanches, Cheyenne, Kiowa, and Osage with them. All young bucks, hungry for war honors."

Captain Reagan had blanched at mention of the slaughter in the village. Family legend, the dark side at least, had it that some Cherokee blood flowed in his veins. It came from Chief Bowles and his New Freedonia colony in the early days of Texas. He repressed his anger and remained impassive as he spoke casually.

"If we're not pressed for time, sit down and get some grub in you. As soon as we've eaten, we'll move out."

Holten had no appetite. He knew, though, that he had to eat to regain strength, so he forced food into himself, thinking of the screaming children.

The attack on the Cherokee village had brought only a little glory to the raiders. Fighting was a way of life to these hard-bitten men of the plains. A lot more fiery liquor made the affair count for more. In their camp, sheltered on one side by the high bank of a creek, the war party celebrated.

"I will go with you, War Moon, to Texas or anywhere, to kill white men," one Osage shouted. All the other warriors joined in as they sprawled about the crude camp, swilling whiskey and picketing the horses they had stolen.

"Those among you who hesitated to go and get their brothers from others camps, go now. Take the guns you need." War Moon pointed to the pile of weapons Barker had left behind when he hastily departed the previous night. "Gather your people."

"We will attack the white man's house they call Fort Sill!" Cold Wind shouted.

"No. Not yet," War Moon counseled. "First we will find the ranger chief with his men and we will lead them east, then wipe them out."

Eli inched up through the sparse grama grass. Silently, the twenty-one Texas Rangers followed him.

The rangers practiced an old ploy they dearly loved. Quietly and patiently they crawled deeper into the tall groundcover, closer to the warriors. The nomadic Plains' tribes had never learned to set sentries out around their villages. Even repeated experience, like Custer's slaughter on the Washita, could not get them to practice this basic tenet of warfare. What they wouldn't think to do in their own hoops, though, they did on the warpath. Unfortunately, none of the lookouts noticed the approaching Texans.

A stream, swollen and thick with debris, surged noisily to the south with perhaps two hundred yards between it and the warriors' bonfire. Open, bare ground lay to the west and the rangers came in from the north and east. It effectively trapped the raiders in a weak position.

Eli lay close enough to the camp to hear War Moon, whom he recognized as the one who had given him Louise, talking in an angry, drunken voice. Though the war leader stumbled through several dialects, few that Holten recognized, he had to get back to English to make sure everyone understood him.

Holten heard the Kiowa-Apache mention *Maman-ti*, then he heard the name, *Tejan*. He remembered the adopted white son of *Maman-ti*, who had disappeared shortly after the owl prophet died. The youth had been the prophet's main pupil and had been initiated into the Buffalo Medicine Lodge at a young age.

At one time, *Tejan* had been rescued, or captured, by a Lt. Frank Baldwin and three army scouts. Their prisoner spoke perfect English and yet said he didn't know any name other than *Tejan*. Baldwin had said the young white man had the red hair of an Irishman and was about eighteen years of age. The youth seemed to be glad to be rescued, yet later he escaped and rejoined his tribe, only to disappear from their number and never be heard from again. Eli saw a connection.

Red Owl had to be *Tejan*, red meaning his hair, and with his heritage he'd be able to gather the many tribes together who had worshipped, loved, and feared *Mamanti*, the Kiowa medicine man, for a new war of revenge and powerful medicine.

The dancing and reveling went on most of the night, while the rangers dozed and conserved their strength, waiting for the light. They had brought their blankets along, knowing how cold the ground could be in the spring.

The false dawn broke and woke the Texans. They moved in even closer. Most of the Indians had passed out or rolled up in their buffalo robes.

As the real light began to filter through, the warriors stirred.

Captain Reagan rose to one knee, his broad-shouldered figure appearing above the grass like a specter in the fresh pink rays of dawn, the bloated red disc of the sun behind him. His opening shot cracked into the mouth of one Osage, who still stumbled around the camp, vaguely dancing to an unheard drum.

The drunken brave leaped into the air from the impact and started a new shuffle on the ground, one to accompany his own death.

Before the brave had fallen, though, the entire detachment fired in a phalanx of pointed yellow lightning, white smoke billowing out across the plains.

Fifteen

Most of the warriors never escaped from their sleeping robes.

Black, sooty-edged holes burst on the soft-cured buffalo hides, and the occupants jerked and twitched their way into death. A few braves coiled out and, though wounded, started returning fire with their new Winchesters.

The withering accuracy of the rangers, however, plowed the camp like sod-busters getting a field ready for planting. A Comanche let out a battle cry. For his trouble, he caught one .44-40 round in his right eye and another in his throat. Three bloody mushrooms erupted across his chest before he had a chance to fall.

Most of the other warriors rolled to the west into the open field. The rangers advanced closer to the camp, though they never left the concealment of the grass. They continued a merciless fire that scythed the hostiles time and again. If the renegades stood or kneeled, the rangers shot them down. If they fell and didn't move, the

Texans took target practice on their prone bodies.

War Moon didn't wait to see the outcome. Like a spooked elk, he ran headlong for the swollen creek. With a mighty thrust he cleared the dirty, foam-slicked water. An older Osage ran to the bank and tried to do the same. He landed near the far edge and began scrambling for safety. A tug of the current knocked his legs out from under him.

For a moment it looked like the aged warrior would still make it. Then a stump of a tree swirled down and cracked into the side of the Osage's head. It ripped an ear off and stuck a six-inch long root through an eye and into his brain. The brave's blood stained the brown water.

Red Pony leaped to a horse and grabbed several spare ones. He picked up Cold Wind and, though both were wounded, made a break to the west until they found a spot in the creek they dared to cross.

The rangers' fusillade didn't let up until nothing in the hostile camp moved.

Carefully, the rangers snaked into the clearing and gingerly checked for life in the fallen Indians. Thacker picked up one of the hostiles' rifles.

"Look at this," he growled. "Winchesters! Brand, spanking new ones."

"More of Red Owl's magic, I suppose," Reagan answered with a grim smile.

"Did you hear any of what War Moon was talking about, captain?" Eli asked.

"It kept switching from one dialect to another too quickly for me," the captain admitted. "My hearing isn't what it used to be, either."

"I think Red Owl is *Tejan*, son of *Maman-ti*," Eli revealed. "And that's powerful medicine."

Reagan recalled the story of *Maman-ti* and grimaced. "Real magic?" he asked, uncertain as to what underlay such stories. "So he knows everything the rangers are

174

doing down in the Panhandle, no matter what we do?"

Well versed in the ways of Indian magic, Holten gave the captain a troubled expression and a slight shrug. "I wouldn't doubt it and I think we had better not waste any more time getting back there. They also said something about finding the ranger captain and leading us deeper into Indian territory, away from Texas."

"They knew I was in the Nations?" A look of consternation flashed quickly across Reagan's face, then disappeared in a scowl. "We've got a beautiful two-day ride ahead of us then. Palo Duro Canyon and Charlie Goodnight are the closest big target for Red Owl. Let's get started."

War Moon spotted his two wounded brothers hurrying away from the bloody field. He ran along the bank, trying to keep them in sight. When they crossed, he ran up to them, helping Red Pony ease Cold Wind off his mount.

"How did they find us?" the youthful warrior gasped, blood flowing freely from his shoulder wound.

"Do not dwell on it," War Moon advised. "Red Owl said it would not be easy for us." The war chief inspected the hole in Cold Wind's thigh. "The bullet passed through. We must find some proper plants to stuff your wounds with, then wrap them tightly."

"We have to locate a place to hide and gain strength as well," Red Pony added.

"No," Cold Wind gasped. "We must get back to Red Owl and warn him the rangers will ride toward Texas now."

The hostiles who laid siege to the XIT ranch house moved through outlying buildings, some of which they set afire. They aimed carefully and peppered the main structure with lead. Here and there, one of them threw up his arms and fell in a spreading pool of blood. Dead cowboys lay sprawled in the dooryard, ignored by all except big, blue-green flies which hovered over the corpses in dark clouds.

Black-Cloud-Full-of-Lights, the warrior in charge of the assault, stood on a ridge and watched through field glasses. He sensed someone behind him and turned, expecting to see one of his counselors. Instead, he looked into the cold, blue eyes of the prophet. Red Owl! His mysterious appearance sent a chill down Black-Cloud's spine.

"The ploy to draw the rangers off to the west was only partially successful," Red Owl started, without greeting his fellow Kiowa-Apache. "Goodnight and all his men came back. Still, the rangers themselves stay out far to the west and War Moon has Captain Reagan occupied in the Indian territory. He also sent me word that he has found the tribes there receptive to our call to war. He has directed many of them to come straight to us here, to storm the ranch."

"Will they come in time?" Red Owl's lieutenant inquired. "Surely one of the other bands of rangers will become suspicious."

"I prophecy a victory here," Red Owl said through his head ornament. His voice sounded hollow and bigger than life. He looked away a bit. "Though not quite as I had hoped. I cannot quite say . . . exactly. . . ." The medicine man slipped into silence, then snapped his head back.

"I need ten of the bravest men you can spare." The prophet's voice grew powerful again. "They will go and draw the rangers to the west always further out, even into New Mexico, so they will pose no threat to us here."

"I shall pick the men myself," Black-Cloud-Full-of-

Lights answered.

"I will stay with you here," Red Owl added, then turned silently and stared down the slope.

War Moon readied his knife as the soft steps of men came closer. The other warriors clutched their weapons as they hid in the depression that previous floods had dug into the wall of the wash. Though the possibility of the water's suddenly rising made the hideout dangerous, the threat of the approaching humans had forced the three Kiowa-Apaches to hide.

Soft shuffling came closer. The braves tensed to die, then someone called out.

"War Moon, is that you?"

The war leader straightened up, hesitated, then whispered softly. "Who is it that calls on War Moon?"

"I am Winter Oak, a Cheyenne you sent out to gather my brothers."

The three warriors sighed, then broke out laughing as they stumbled out of the hole. Winter Oak looked at them strangely. He had forty braves with him, Osage and Cheyenne, grown bitter with exile in the Nations.

"I saw your animals up here with the markings of the Kiowa-Apache," Winter Oak said, explaining his search for them.

"We were attacked by Texas Rangers as we slept," War Moon admitted. A grumble ran through the many mounted warriors.

"Listen to me," War Moon yelled out. "Even as we speak, my leader, Red Owl, is attacking the place where the white men stay in the canyon they call Palo Duro. There is much glory and many *coups* to be counted there. Come with us and we will gain some of the glory."

The new men silently glanced at each other nervously.

177

To come to a massacre and be expected to keep riding into battle seemed unreasonable. Several made as to turn away.

"Remember the Battle of the Washita?" the Kiowa-Apache pressed. "There *Maman-ti* rescued many Cheyenne women and children from Yellow Hair's men. He was a Kiowa and a cousin to our people. Red Owl is his son! Will you not answer *Maman-ti*'s son when he calls you?"

"The Battle of the Washita was a long time ago," a Cheyenne brave answered.

"Look at the rifles in your hands," War Moon urged. "Your brother Winter Oak brought those to you from Red Owl. The prophet has given you a gift for joining him. If you have changed your minds, then leave the weapons with me so I can give them to braver men than you."

The discontented warriors fell silent. The Winchesters had brought them to Red Owl's call. The Winchesters would keep them there.

After breakfast, Eli and the rangers galloped on, crossing the north fork of the Red River near the Texas line. The ground showed signs of where some of the Kiowa-Apaches had escaped.

"Should we follow them?" Thacker suggested.

"So long as they seem to be heading southwest, we might as well," Reagan answered.

Half an hour later, they came to a wash and Eli pushed his hat back on his head. He uttered a tuneless whistle.

"Damn," he cursed. No one had to explain his explosion. Every man there could see the stamped and shredded ground where it had been torn up by many unshod ponies. Holten figured at least forty.

178

"Soon as we kill them, they spring up again," Thacker sighed.

"More powerful medicine," Reagan added.

"What do we do?" Eli asked.

"We follow these new tracks. Only this time we wait until they get to Red Owl before jumping them. Kill or capture him and we bring this whole thing to a halt."

"It won't be no trouble following this one, captain," Thacker said. "These tracks are aiming straight toward Palo Duro Canyon."

Another shocked expression shot across the captain's face before disappearing behind a rugged look of purpose. "Tony!" he cried out. "Ben!"

Two rangers pulled up beside him.

"Yes, sir," they answered in unison.

"I want you to head back to our main camp and get every healthy ranger started toward the XIT Ranch, *pronto*."

"Damnit, Duke," Tony protested. "That could take an awful long time. Menardville is a long way off."

"If I know Charles Goodnight," Reagan replied, "it's gonna take a long time to take that ranch house. Now get."

The two riders took off. Before they were even out of sight, Eli spotted a buggy charging toward them.

"Stop!" Jeremiah Turpin shouted. In his wagon sat his wife and in the back, Louise's tear-stained face looked sadly over the side. "Hold on!"

Turpin pulled the lathered horses up and leaped from his vehicle. He turned toward Holten, the first man he recognized.

"Take her back!" he pleaded.

"Louise?" Reagan asked.

"The whore! The vile temptress of Babylon." Turpin danced with his anger and anxiety. "She's a plague, a scourge, a diseased creature that must be kept from the gentle red men at the reservation . . . or every squaw will throw her husband's belongings from her tipi and divorce him in their pagan ways. This wretched slattern is driving our converts away from salvation."

"I have no idea what you mean," Reagan stated calmly, ignorant of Louise's unusual nature. "You will please explain what you're raving about."

"I can't speak of such things in front of my wife," Turpin wailed.

"My husband may not," April rose and said, "but I will." She pointed at Louise, who blanched and cringed from the accusing finger.

"This harlot came into our house, bathed and accepted the clean clothes we offered her. We let her in out of the goodness of our hearts. And how does she repay us? She scampered down to the dwellings of our brother red men and seduced the young boys into the woods to take turns on her in fornication and sodomy. Having sinned these young men into submission, the shameless tramp went to the camp and took over a lodge, where she invited every man and boy in the village to cohabit with her."

"The line wrapped around the lodge," Turpin blubbered. "Twice!"

"She received their evil members any way, anywhere," April continued. "Worse, she actually *enjoyed* it . . . gloried in it! She is a threat to God and our mission to the Children of Nature."

Eli rode to the back of the wagon to find tears flowing freely from Louise's eyes as she sobbed softly and hid her face from the crowd of rangers, who looked her way hungrily. He left his horse and sat down next to her. The young girl looked up, her eyes swollen and full of misery.

"She's right, Eli," Louise choked out. "It's some kind of sickness. I can't help myself. Ever since I was a little bit of a girl, I see a man, any man, an' all I want to do is

180

pleasure with 'im."

"There, there, Louise," Eli murmured in consolation as he wrapped an arm around her shoulders. "You're not sick."

"Oh, yes, I am," she blubbered. "Here I am all tear-stained and miserable an' all I can think is how I'd like to have fun with you right now."

Eli glanced around at the rangers, young and old alike, trying not to overhear the conversation. They heard enough from the Turpins, though. Some of them shifted uncomfortably on their saddles or tugged at their tight trousers.

"Not here, Louise," he cautioned, feeling a growing response of his own.

"I don't care where," she blubbered. "All these boys could join in if they wanted."

"Say," Turpin snipped as his eyes focused through the rage that had blinded him. "You men are not soldiers. You're Texas Rangers."

"Yes, sir," Reagan admitted with a sigh.

"Rangers in the sacred land of the red man, set aside by *Washington*!" Turpin wailed in rekindled anger.

"I have a legal right to pursue criminals and raiders into other states and territories. That's clearly stated in the statute books and the United States Constitution, God love it."

"The laws of the federal government and the rights of the Indians in the Nations supercede the rights of the states or that antiquated document of rebellion you referred to." Jeremiah sucked new air into his lungs to prolong his harangue.

"I ain't gonna argue with you, Mr. Turpin," Reagan snapped. "I'm headed back into Texas now, pursuing the Kiowa-Apaches who brought me into the territory."

"Then I insist we go along," the Indian agent snarled. "I will not let you harm the innocent children you have

181

frightened off their lands. I intend to protect the noble red men from the criminal nature of all whites."

"Go suck eggs, Turpin," Les Thacker growled. "The Kiowa-Apaches come outta New Mexico and the corner of Colorado and you've got a lotta goddamned nerve claimin' them as your own."

"Ease off, Les," Captain Reagan advised.

"I should think so," Turpin returned prissily. "Now, I demand—"

"Demand all you like, but you'll do as I say," the ranger captain warned.

Eli unwound Louise's tightening grip on his rigid organ and crawled backward out of the wagon. He sincerely hoped none of the rangers would notice. The girl looked shattered as well as humiliated.

"If you want to come along," Reagan went on, "that's fine. You keep your mouths shut, do as I say and the young lady will remain in the wagon. She'll be more comfortable."

"Never! This slut will no longer sully the presence of decent folk, my wife, and myself," Turpin stated flatly.

Duke Reagan had taken all he could from this sanctimonious hypocrite. He pulled out his seven-inch barreled .45 Colt Frontier, stuck the muzzle in Turpin's ever widening mouth and cocked the hammer. A sweet, gentle smile broke out on his face.

"When I joined the rangers before the war, I promised my daddy that I wouldn't kill an unarmed man, that not being sporting. But I'm willing to make an exception in your case, Mr. Turpin." The ranger's smile faded. "I will not tolerate that kind of language in the presence of a child . . . no matter how, uh, precocious she happens to be. Have I made myself clear?"

Gulping the taste of gun oil, Turpin nodded and Reagan drew his weapon back.

"You can follow if you like, but we're riding hard to

catch up with these raiders. And don't mistreat the girl."

Wilderspin stirred from his blanket, looked around groggily in the half light of dawn, then rose to find out if any coffee still brewed over the fire. He figured they'd head back, whether Meyers came with bad news or not. It seemed to the ranger officer there might be bigger problems back in Menardville and those scattered communities around it. They still had to figure out how Mulock and its men had been wiped out without more of a fight.

From the west the whining noise of a ricocheting bullet filled the lieutenant's ears, followed by the loud crack of a rifle. Wilderspin ducked low and drew his six-gun. The other rangers rolled out of their bedrolls, hauled out their Winchesters and crawled on their bellies for cover. In the ominous silence that followed, they tried to locate where the fire came from.

A warrior, a Kiowa-Apache by his dress and ornaments, rode headlong at them. He reined his horse in a good fifty yards away, took a good look at the twenty white men coming at him on foot and sped off the way he came. Mercilessly he thumped the flanks of his pony to urge more speed.

"There's gotta be more where he came from," Wilderspin yelled out. "Gather up your horses and we'll go after them."

The rangers feverishly saddled their mounts, took jerky and cold biscuits from their saddlebags and in ten minutes started off after the lone hostile.

Sixteen

War Moon and the forty braves who followed him reached the XIT Ranch an hour before dark. The greeting they received pulled away the warriors who pressed down on the cowboys pinned in the adobe headquarters. For a short while it relieved the merciless fire Goodnight and his men had suffered for a second day. From the shattered windows of the structure, however, the longtime cowman could see tomorrow would be much worse.

"Enough water to last through tomorrow," Eddie Quaid reported. "Enough ammunition, plenty of food. Lots of our people are wounded, though. If we don't get some real doctorin' out here, I don't know what'll happen to them."

"What the fuck is taking that goddamned Wilderspin so long?" Goodnight snapped. "I pray to Jesus he's not still chasing those disappearin' Injuns."

"It might've been a feint, Mr. Goodnight," Quaid suggested. "Someone might be drawing Wilderspin off."

"That's what I was thinking," Loving sighed. "Tie up the local rangers while we shoot it out with these savages."

"We won't be shooting for much fucking longer," the magnificently profane rancher warned. "With all those extra pigfuckers I see out there, those boys could overrun us real damn quick."

The warriors greeted the arriving Cheyenne, Comanches, and Osage with shouts and battle cries, extra ammunition and jugs of whiskey.

"We have counted many *coups*," Black-Cloud-Full-of-Lights cried. "We have gained much wealth from the buildings around the white man's last holdout. Tomorrow, we will trade for more ammunition from Barker. But before we do that, we will wipe out the white men in the dried mud lodge they hide in."

The warriors cried out their glory, as Red Owl watched from a distance. His eyes took fire as his hope rose in his followers' faith and enthusiasm. He knew that ahead of them lay troubled times, with mixed victories and hard labor. The owl had told him that. But if he could get the white warrior, Tall Bear, killed, his problems would be controllable.

Holten and Thacker peered over the tall grass and studied the throng of dancing, drunken Indians. The throbbing of a lone tom-tom matched their pounding pulses.

"There must be eighty to a hundred of them," Wild Man gasped.

"Pretty good counting, Les," Eli complimented. "I figure about the same."

"What are we gonna do?" Thacker asked.

"If we got back to Captain Reagan real quick," Holten speculated, "we might be able to get in position and jump them in the morning."

"Like we did in the territory!" Les whispered hoarsely with enthusiasm.

"It'll be close," Holten warned, "but after watching you boys the last time we got in some shooting, I'll lay odds on you rangers anytime."

Les Thacker beamed with pride. From a distance, Red Pony, who had fallen back because of his wounds, had seen the two dark figures sneaking through the grass. He followed and now lay no more than five feet away. He spoke no English, though, as the two white men inched away, he knew instinctively that the pair had seen how many followers Red Owl had here and what they planned to do. In the moonlight, Red Pony recognized the one who called himself Tall Bear.

Two warriors dragged a white man into the presence of the red one, who sat on the hill watching the celebration below. The medicine man looked up, studied the white's face, then waved the two braves away.

"Did you kill Eli Holten and the ranger?" Red Owl asked.

For a moment, Ike Lampbertson hesitated, swallowed and sighed.

"No," he finally answered. The prophet sat frozen on his perch, staring deadly cold at the gunslinger.

"Uh . . . me and my partner jumped them on the way down. He blasted the ranger but Holten pulled his gun fast and shot my man dead. Thacker recovered."

"This is a bad sign," Red Owl stated flatly. "I had a dream that the white warrior from the north would come and stop me."

"What the hell kind of game you pulling, Red?" Ike

demanded, his voice trembling despite his challenging question. "This some kind of deal to rob a bank or hold up a train?"

Red Owl continued to stare death at the white man, sending shivers of fear down the shootist's spine. Then the medicine chief smiled and a new burst of thrilling chills shuddered Lampbertson.

"You will wait until I have decided how you shall kill Holten," Red Owl ordered.

Red Pony, his wound wrapped in grass and leaves, stumbled up the hill and to Red Owl's feet.

"Prophet," he greeted. "Two white men have been spying on us."

Red Owl sprang to his feet. "Who? Where?"

"A ranger and the one who says he is an Oglala warrior from the north, Tall Bear."

War Moon loped up the hill after Red Pony. "Is it true?" he asked his young follower. "The rangers close in on us?"

"If we hurry, we might catch the two before they reach the other white men," Red Pony suggested.

"No," Red Owl stated bluntly. "I have a better plan."

Red Owl issued terse orders and the camp exploded into action.

Riding Wolf's men, mostly Kiowa-Apaches and Comanches, would stay where they were, looking natural, yet ready for the rangers' sneak attack. War Moon gathered up his other followers, among them Osage and Cheyenne. Red Pony and Cold Wind, though wounded, insisted on coming along.

"Get behind the rangers," Red Owl directed as the braves mounted up. "Come up from behind. Scare off their horses and then we will pick them off as they had planned to do to us."

"We will have to be careful not to catch each other in a crossfire," War Moon warned.

"We will favor this hill over here," Riding Wolf instructed. "If you will come up from behind, and the rangers will be on top, there is much less chance of shooting each other."

Forty glory-drunk warriors rode off, leaving the other Indians as decoys.

Meanwhile, Red Owl started to change from his medicine clothes. More sparks of genius came to him and he planned a final, brutal twist to the death of Company D.

"We have 'em," Reagan chortled when he had heard Holten's report. "We'll catch the whole lot of them sitting over the XIT."

"We'll hit 'em like we hit War Moon, out in the open," Thacker added.

"There's a whole lot more of them this time than before," Eli countered as the rangers ate a cold supper and checked their weapons and ammo.

"We've been up against big odds before, Eli," Reagan answered. "We're not afraid of being outnumbered. I know you're probably sick of hearing Texans boast and brag, but I've got twenty great men here, not to mention the element of surprise. We come howling over the top of that hill and they won't know what's hitting them. We'll sound like a hundred men an' go through them like a dose of salts. I haven't lost one yet and I don't plan to. We'll have Goodnight's boys on one side and us on the other. Thacker, you have to sneak down to the ranch house and let them know we're coming. They have to open up when they hear us attack."

"I'll go right now," Thacker offered. He turned like a shot and leaped to the back of his painted horse.

"Now, you sneak in, don't just ride through them, Wild man," Reagan shouted after the youthful Texan.

"We don't want to make Red Owl suspicious."

Eli nervously looked northeast. He'd done that since he and Thacker had returned from reconnoitering the Palo Duro Canyon. Reagan, too, glanced in that direction and read Holten's mind.

"You're worried about that Louise and the Turpins."

"Louise at least," the scout corrected. "I think of those people mistreating that poor little thing and I get pretty mad."

"Go on back there and make sure she's all right," Reagan suggested. "See that they're settled for the night. Maybe even rig it so Turpin can't get here until after sunrise." The captain sighed. "I believe that idiot when he said he planned to keep us from attacking Red Owl. He *believes* his own lies. Such men are dangerous."

"I'll insure they don't get near you, Duke," Eli promised. "But I'm gonna be with you boys when the shooting starts."

"Wouldn't have it any other way, Eli," Reagan chortled through a sandstorm in his throat.

The scout backtracked the rangers' trail, knowing that the Easterner would have to follow those tracks in order not to get lost. To Holten's surprise, he discovered the Turpins only two hours behind the rangers.

The two horses pulling the buckboard frothed at their bits. The fanatic-eyed Jeremiah Turpin plied a whip across their backs. He stood with the reins in hand as the wagon bounced brutally along the barely worn trail the rangers on horseback had followed. The two determined members of the Society of Friends on the driver's box glared hostilely at the approaching rider.

"You had better back off that whip or you're going to kill your horses," Eli warned by way of a greeting.

"Better these dumb beasts than the Children of Nature you intend to butcher," April Turpin hissed defiantly.

Louise peeked over the driver's box as Eli looked to the

west. The glow of the sunset dwindled quickly.

"You've got no more light. You have to stop for the night."

"Then the attack will happen before the morning!" Jeremiah triumphantly calculated. He drew his whip back and struck across the flanks of the animals in front of him.

"These horses aren't going to make it at this rate," Holten angrily shouted as the beasts stumbled forward in the glowering dusk. "At least stop long enough to let them catch their strength. They'll be dead in an hour and you'll never get to War Moon."

"Although a heathen, thee speak the truth, Mr. Holten," April Turpin told him.

Jeremiah stopped his flailing, hesitated, then sat back down.

"There's a small stream up ahead," Holten urged. "You can water your animals and I'll help you wipe them down. Walk 'em to the water so they won't drink all heated and founder."

Turpin seemed to come to a decision.

"Two hours' rest for the horses and ourselves, then we will press on."

"You can get something to eat," Eli added. "I'll help."

The horses drank voluminously and the scout only hoped they would get enough time to rest before they started. Holten felt sure that once the Turpins let their own exhaustion sink in, they'd settle down for the night. With Louise silently watching from near the wagon, Eli moved up to a slight rise and started a fire. He hauled out the limited supplies that the Indian agent had thrown into their transportation.

"We do not require much food," April explained as she and her husband led the horses and wagon up from the low ground. "We are fed by the Holy Spirit."

"That's good, because I'm going out to snare a rabbit

191

for me and Louise. You can eat the beans and sugar."

Holten trotted off toward the east. He hated rabbit. "A man who eats rabbit talks to himself," he'd been told once. "And a man who talks to himself, lies." Still, he needed to catch something quickly. He didn't want the Turpins running off while he hunted.

Louise ran up to the scout. "Let me go with you a little ways," she asked, then leaned close to his ear. "I need to go pee."

The two trotted out a few steps and the girl demurely ducked into the bushes while Holten continued on.

Suddenly, from the camp behind him, Eli heard the war whoops of Indians. He froze, clutched his Winchester close to him, then gingerly started back toward the camp, working around to the south.

From his vantage point and cover, Eli saw the attack had ended abruptly. The scout couldn't understand the conversation going on between the chief he recognized as War Moon and the Indian agent. They seemed on friendly terms, though.

"We did not know it was you, White Peace Pipe," War Moon apologized in imperfect Kiowa. "We thought perhaps you were some of the Texas Rangers, whom we seek." The Kiowa-Apache laughed. "Tomorrow we will wipe the Texans and their leader, Reagan, out! We will hang their scalps on our *coup* sticks and cut their balls off to remember this great day."

Suddenly the warrior froze. His change proved too subtle for the agent and his wife to see. Eli, however, immediately realized War Moon stared past the wagon.

Out of the gloom that the fire couldn't reach stepped a wild-eyed creature, staring hungrily at the many assembled warriors. All those sweaty, nearly naked bodies, Louise thought, as she came around the wagon. All those young, handsome, deeply tanned creatures who could give what she could never get enough of.

War Moon took an imperceptible step back, while Red Pony and Cold Wind gasped. Then memory stirred in the Kiowa-Apache boy's mind and the front of Red Pony's loincloth began to bulge outward. Unaware of the new circumstances, Turpin bravely came to his full stature, and in Kiowa, carefully translating to carry all the meaning of the words, Jeremiah quoted the Bible.

"Thou shalt not kill!" the Quaker boomed. His voice softened. "You must love the white man. If you kill those evil ones tomorrow, though they deserve your wrath, you and your soul will pay the price."

A horny Louise took a step back. Trembles of fear— something these warriors had not known before meeting Louise Van Pelton—etched across the three Kiowa-Apaches' faces. Meanwhile, those who had come with them watched on in stoic ignorance.

War Moon felt the eyes of the others watching. He straightened up and spoke coolly in Kiowa-Apache, a language the Cheyennes and Osage, for the most part, couldn't understand.

"We will not attack the rangers," War Moon announced. "We believe only in peace and wish only to live in peace. We will do as you ask, White Peace Pipe, only . . . *don't let the Yellow Bush get to us!*"

"What did he mean, 'Yellow Bush'?" April asked her husband after he had translated the term into English.

"I believe he means Satan or sin," Jeremiah replied thoughtfully. "Or perhaps his own moral weakness." Then, in Kiowa, in which he was more perfectly versed, Jeremiah intoned, "You must fight the Yellow Bush."

"No!" War Moon protested. "I do not wish to fight it, but to avoid it."

With as much dignity as the situation allowed, War Moon turned and ordered the other warriors to mount and ride.

The sound of many hoofs rumbling off made Holten

duck deeper into his cover. When finally the Indians'
exit faded, Holten gingerly moved into the camp.

"There!" Jeremiah boomed triumphantly, wiping his
long, white fingers together in a gesture of washing.
"Peace and love triumph. The word of God has brought
about peace. I have saved the rangers!"

Seventeen

". . . who only need love and understanding to stop these minor social upheavals," Jeremiah intoned piously as Eli feverishly checked Sonny, cinching his saddle down and stripping off everything he didn't need.

Turpin straightened up, unconsciously guilty of the sin of pride and condescendingly added, "The Society of Friends way is the true way! If thou speak as if to a child with love and tolerance, thou can reason with the savages until they can make these moral decisions for themselves. No rod nor whip can beat goodness into any man. Only pacifism, humility, and rejection of all violent things will free these Children of Nature from their moral void."

"A good kick in the ass would help," Holten muttered under his breath, then answered Turpin curtly. "You stay here, Turpin. War Moon might stumble onto Reagan's tracks and follow them in."

"That's what they *planned* to do," Turpin corrected smugly. "They intended to come up from behind and wipe the rangers out to the man! But because of my intervention, War Moon renounced such terrible things and seeks only to live in peace."

"I'll believe that when horses lay eggs and chickens fly to the moon," the scout growled. He shot a look back at the Quaker, to determine if Turpin actually believed all he had said. Sure enough, the scout could read Turpin's mind like a book through his candidly open, pale blue eyes. Jeremiah really swallowed War Moon's line.

"You, ah, don't mind if I run ahead and tell Captain Reagan how you saved his life?" Holten inquired dryly.

"Go ahead. I will stop *him* as well."

Holten grabbed the saddle horn and pulled himself up into the seat.

"Don't leave me here, Eli," Louise suddenly wailed. Holten thought he heard the slightest tremble in her voice. The scout figured, for all their talk of love, the Quaker couple must have treated the young girl shabbily. For a man who had no trouble reading other men, Eli seemed to miss the hunger that went with the tremble in Louise's soft appeal. Out of pity, he reached an arm down to her and pulled her up behind him.

With a stiff-kneed bounce, Sonny shot forward, little Louise entwining her arms around Eli's chest to stay on. The firelight receded rapidly.

In moments the night closed with a vengeance and Holten could only trot forward, trusting the wise and careful Sonny to avoid gullies and washes. Left to his own devices, the mighty beast would keep them on the trail until they came to where the rangers' horses hid. The scout chaffed at the slow pace.

Louise chaffed for things other than speed. As she bounced energetically on Sonny, her legs splayed wide across the flanks, her thoughts went to her favorite thing. War Moon and the two others, plus plenty more, all muscular and sweaty in their skimpy breechcloths, worked her toward sensual hysteria. Jiggling around behind this full hulk of a man, who had resisted her feminine wiles earlier, drove her over the brink.

To Holten's sudden shock, Louise's hands worked down to his crotch. She slipped up on the cantle of the high back saddle and ground herself hard against his back. Her sweet-scented breath came hot in his ear.

"Stop, Eli!" she cried, unbridled passion bursting on her. "Stop and make love with me. We'll spend the whole night lying with each other. I'll be good for you, Eli, I swear I will!"

"Get ahold of yourself, girl!" Holten hissed back at her, trying to pry her diminutive fingers from his slowly rousing organ. Like a wild animal, she tore at him, totally out of control.

"I need you!" she gurgled. "I want you! I've got to have you!"

"Keep your voice down," Eli whispered hoarsely as they jolted along. "We have to get to Captain Reagan and warn him about War Moon. If those warriors are around, they'll hear you."

"Oh," she cried. "All those sweaty, beautiful Injuns. I swear, Eli, if you don't soothe me right now, I'm going to scream."

"Don't scream!" Holten urged and knew what had to be done.

Out of sheer desperation, Holten stopped. He swung off Sonny, the creature on his back holding on like some wild animal. He slid his trousers off, all the while warring with his conscience. The girl grappled down to his crotch and his already lengthening shaft.

"Oh, Eli, are you ever ready!" Louise rejoiced. While she knelt and took him into her mouth, Eli sighed with resignation and threw his pants across the saddle.

"No, Louise, we have to keep moving," Holten told her. A shock ran through him as the rough surface of her

197

energetic tongue rubbed around and around on the sensitive tip of his pulsating manhood. A shock of another kind flashed through his mind as he realized how much he was enjoying it and how incredibly good Louise was at what she did.

"I mean it," he repeated with a hint of regret in his voice. "We've got to go." He gently disengaged Louise from his swollen prong, remounted Sonny, then pulled the crazed girl back up with him. This time he sat her facing backwards in front of him.

She instantly impaled herself on Eli's fleshy lance, even as Holten touched heels to Sonny's flanks.

"Aye-e-e!" Louise cried as she worked herself down inside the tight saddle, until the scout's rigid phallus dug deeply inside her dripping cavern. Suddenly Louise became very quiet, except for her gulping gasps of ecstasy.

Penetrated by Holten in front, the saddle horn ground into her rump with each trotting step Sonny took. The combination sent rivulets of delight through her young body, tingling her scalp. She pulled her dress down so her breasts swayed against the scout's buckskin shirt.

As the muscular ridges along her burning passage contracted and released in time with Sonny's steady gait, Eli grew dizzy with the delirious pleasure Louise brought him. He gasped and groaned and his hips began to thrust to the same rhythm. In a tiny, distant, sober corner of his brain, Holten hoped to God no one, including the Indians, would see him like this. He also prayed he could look himself in the mirror again.

Leroy Barker walked over to where Red Owl changed, dressing for more action.

"Red, we gotta talk," Leroy stated.

"Speak," the prophet demanded. "I rush to bring the

rangers in the west here, so that they might be slaughtered as soon as we are done with the XIT and Charlie Goodnight."

"I've stood by you every inch of the way."

"For a price," Red Owl reminded.

"I nearly got caught by the rangers twice," Leroy continued more heatedly. "Once on the road from New Mexico and once out there in the Indian territory. If I'd waited until War Moon finished with those Cherokee, they would'a caught me there, Red. Damnit! I snuck a horde of your killers into Mulock in the back of my wagon so's they could take out all the fighting men before they knew what hit them."

"From what Black-Cloud-Full-of-Lights told me, you enjoyed the attack, especially raping several of the women in Mulock."

"I didn't kill no one," Leroy nearly shouted. He glanced around to where two young braves watched and lowered his voice. "I just want some guarantees, that's all."

"Guarantees?" Red Owl repeated scornfully.

"Yeah," the trader answered nervously. "When I first got tied up with you, I figured to make a few bucks. I think now, though, you're actually gonna do it. You're going to take this part of the country back."

"You are wiser than I thought," the medicine man commented.

"I'm with you, now, Red Owl," Barker continued. "I've thrown my lot in with you. But when the time comes, you aren't going to kill me, too, are you?"

Red Owl rose to his full stature and rested a hand on Barker's shoulder.

"Hear me, trader, for I will speak the truth. When we have routed the army and killed off the rangers and we are wiping out each white man's village to cleanse our land of their presence," Red Owl leaned toward Leroy and patted him on the side of the face. "You had better run like hell."

Louise shivered with the convolutions that washed over her. She sighed with the overwhelming satisfaction the moment brought. Her sexual frenzy faded with her strength. Nothing had ever been quite like that before and . . . and it had been . . . wonderful! She rested with her lower body jammed tightly against Eli's sweaty pelvis, his huge, softening member plunged deeply inside her, and sighed with utter delight.

"You . . . you made me so happy, Eli," she panted out. "But . . . you wore me out."

Eli looked to heaven and said a prayer of thanks. He needed all his strength, which he felt the talented young girl siphoning off so rapidly. Besides, the rangers' horses had come into sight. With delicacy, he dislodged the nearly slumbering girl from his shaft.

"Oh, Eli," she sighed as he pulled free. "I've *never* felt like this before. If I had to die right now, I'd go fulfilled."

"Louise," the scout whispered back, his vexation returning. "What am I going to do with you? How can I do right by you?"

She reached down shyly and wrapped her fingers around his reddened shaft. "Give me this wonderful thing five, six, seven times a day, dear Eli."

Eli groaned. "I mean about your future."

Louise mumbled something as Holten slipped the dress back over her pert, firm breasts and slid her to the back of the slightly angered, certainly offended, Sonny. Holten couldn't understand what the girl said, only that she might finally *sleep* for a change. He fumbled with his britches and pulled them back on. Only then did he trot down to where the lone guard kept an eye on the rangers' mounts.

"Who goes there?" the Texan hoarsely called out, ready for action.

"Eli Holten," the scout answered.

"Get over here," the young man admonished. "The captain's been waiting for you."

Holten swung down from his horse, then eased Louise to her feet.

"We've got problems, son," Eli told the sentry. "You've got to move the horses. A bunch of braves are sneaking up on your position."

"Holy shit," the ranger hissed back. He pointed to the hill. "The captain is right on top there. You can't miss him. Near that tree."

"Get her inside a blanket." Holten thrust the somnabulant Louise at the Ranger. "And whatever you do, *don't wake her up.*"

Holten mentally prepared himself as he changed from his boots to his Sioux moccasins. He began to think, *what does silence sound like?*

As he climbed the slope, maneuvering around clumps of sage, past rocks and over sand, the crickets didn't miss a beat of their song, snakes that came out to soak up heat from the rocks hardly sensed his steps and knew the intruder had no interest in them. Far off, a loon called from the reeds along the banks of the Red River.

Red Owl only hesitated long enough to turn to Lampbertson.

"I have had a vision," he stated. "I saw a great white warrior come down from the north. He must be stopped."

"Do you have to talk like that?" Ike complained. "We both know you mean Holten. How do you know this guy? You've had a run-in with him before?"

"I have never met Eli Holten," the prophet replied. "And with your help, I never will. Except to spit on his

201

dead body. You will seek him out and kill him. You have been paid. Now earn it!"

"Where the hell are you going now?" Lampbertson demanded.

"Tomorrow, Reagan and his men will be cleaned from the sacred soil of the Kiowa-Apache. I will bring the rangers from the west here to be finished off as well."

Reagan didn't hear the scout until Holten slid in next to him. Still, the captain showed no great alarm or surprise.

"Where ya been?" Duke asked in a soft, sandy whisper. "We attack in a couple of hours."

"I've been dodging Indians, Captain," Holten answered. "The game's over. Red Owl knows we're here. War Moon is coming up behind us right now. I saw them with my own eyes. Turpin told me what they said. Those redskins down front must know what's going on, too. It's a trap."

"Something didn't ring right," Reagan growled back.

"What the hell are we going to do, Captain?" Eli asked.

"You go that way, I'll go to the left. Round up all the boys and have them fall back and to the left on the hillside. Get out of those Indians' way. It's the only chance we've got."

Silently, yet with great speed, Holten squirmed along the ridge, locating each ranger, slapping a hand over each mouth before the man could resist, then whispering the new orders. He avoided discussion, preferring not to tell them too much. They fell back behind the crest and crawled quickly to the left of the rise. In the dark, their progress became marked with growing tension. Courage for them—past the bravado and the boasting—turned out to be wracked with apprehension, though they still did what they were ordered to do.

The blackness of the night, though, hid their movements from War Moon, who led his men in careful stealth up the back side of the promentory. With every step the warriors stabbed with war lance and knife, seeking out the perimeter of the rangers, confident they lay ahead. Yet they did not know for sure where that might be.

Many hours before, Les Thacker had slipped in to the XIT compound as the sun blinded the watching red men and the longest shadows offered him the best cover. He'd slid around corral posts, hugged adobe walls and slithered like a snake across open ground. He passed unsuspecting warriors who only saw the building they sought to overrun. At last he reached the lone structure still in the hands of the cowmen.

At the back entrance, where servants and deliveries ordinarily arrived at the ranch, Wild Man crawled up the wooden steps, cracked open the door and got the double barrels of a scattergun stuck in his face.

Only his eyes looked over the sights of the weapon, staring into those of the man holding the dual messengers of death.

"Boy," Eddie Quail growled coldly. "You don't know how close your brains came to fertilizing the backyard."

"I'm a ranger," Les countered hastily. "And just for spite, I'm gonna save your ass."

Eighteen

The rangers gathered together on the low left side of the oddly steamboat-shaped promentory that stood alone far from the tall, painted walls of Palo Duro Canyon, overlooking the headquarters of the XIT Ranch. The Texans fought exhaustion as their bodies rebelled against the mistreatment they'd received on the trail. Twenty gallant men fell in around their leader as Reagan waited patiently, humming "The Yellow Rose of Texas" softly to himself until all the men could be counted present.

"Good work, Eli," Duke offered with a crinkled smile.

"I sent someone down to make sure the sentry moved the horses," Holten added to his report.

"We moved them just in time," a ranger whispered from the ranks. "I could smell those Injuns closing in on us."

"Now what do we do?" someone inquired.

"We gotta turn this thing around," the captain stated in his gravelly whisper, which carried softly to the attentive ears of his men. "They think we're going to be waiting to jump their decoys down in front, so they're going to bide their time before they attack. When do you figure we'd make the best targets?"

"When we stuck our heads up to open fire on the Injuns down below," Eli volunteered.

"Right," Reagan answered. "And we won't know what to shoot at until they're shooting, will we?"

"What are you suggesting, Duke?" someone asked.

"Some of you boys are gonna have to crawl back out there and open fire. We need decoys, just like War Moon does."

A long silence fell on the gathered men.

"If old Wild Man was here, he'd volunteer, wouldn't he?" Eli asked finally.

"Sure,"Reagan replied. "He's a sucker for the risk."

"Well, then, I'm going." Eli stepped away from the clutch of men. Almost immediately two rangers joined him.

"That should be plenty," Reagan announced, stopping a flourish of motion toward the scout. "You boys spread well out. Holten, you lead the attack. The moment you get maybe two shots off, *you get the hell down and stay there*, like you've been hit. Understand?"

The three men nodded.

"Go," Reagan urged and they slithered off.

Tom Meyers rode headlong into Wilderspin's camp, the sun still not up. "Injuns!" he cried. "All over the XIT Ranch house."

He nearly fell from his overheated horse, hitting the ground and stumbling before the ranger lieutenant caught him. "They hit Charlie Goodnight at home," the ranger scout gasped. "They nearly got me. I'm lucky to be alive."

"How many Indians, Tom?" Wilderspin asked.

"Must be close to eighty."

The other rangers had jumped from their bedrolls and, with the barest facts they overheard, started saddling up their ponies.

"Is Goodnight holding out?"

"Last I saw, they still had the ranch house," Tom answered, sucking for air. "They can't hold for much longer. More Injuns coming in from the territory."

"Let's ride," Wilderspin ordered. He turned back to the scout.

"You wanna rest up a mite and catch up with us when you can?"

Tom hesitated, nodded, then added, "Hurry!"

Wilderspin leaped to the saddle of his mount and silently led the way back toward the Palo Duro.

War Moon had become suspicious. He expected to hear motion at the top of the hill where the rangers should have been. Sunrise would come soon and, if he couldn't locate them, he wouldn't know what to shoot at. So far they had not encountered a single ranger. He wondered if they could already be in position to assault the decoys left so temptingly exposed for them.

His men still sullenly inched up the back slope, and War Moon feared they dwelled on his cowardly retreat in the face of Little Yellow Bush. The Cheyenne and Osage could not know the terror of the white demon, so all he could hope was that glory would vindicate him today.

Suddenly a figure rose in front of them, not ten yards ahead, slightly off to the left. From its form, a burst of light shot away down the front slope and a clap of thunder followed. Two more human shapes rose, and their rifles barked down at the decoys menacing the front of the ranch house.

Yes, the rest of the rangers must have moved further

down the hill, War Moon thought, as he braced his Winchester against his shoulder. Eliminate these three and then rush the rest when they showed themselves, he decided, as he took aim.

Though he had instructed his mixed group of men to silence, to advance bravely but quietly up the reverse slope until the firing started, the hot-blooded young bucks jumped into action at the sound of shots, hooting their war cries and charging headlong up the hill. Cursing their impetuousness, War Moon fired at the closest target.

Eli fell forward into a thicket of mesquite that dotted the hill and the hot lead sliced over him. Immediately he began to crawl to the left, looking to get back to where he'd last seen Captain Reagan. He came across one of the two rangers who had gone out with him.

The glory-seeking youth had been hit in the back of the head, the shoulder, and neck. What flesh still clung to his shoulders had been reduced to a pulpy mass of watery blood and gory gobbets of brain matter.

To Eli's surprise, in the darkness, Captain Reagan had moved at least half of his men down behind the out-thrust "prow" of the eroded formation. As War Moon's braves bounded from the hiding places to charge up the hill, ten rangers appeared behind them and carefully took aim at the silhouetted figures who shouted continuous battle challenges as they raced for the top of the hill.

Next to War Moon, Red Pony suddenly twisted, only a split second after his chest burst outward into pieces, disgorging a fountain before him. Blood and slivers of flesh and bone splattered over his older brother, the war chief. Bitter anguish washed across War Moon's face and he fleetingly recalled that Red Pony had only two hands and four of summers.

Before War Moon could utter the sounds of mourning, or understand what had happened at his rear, more fire opened up on his men from the left flank. Enfiladed now, his warriors, only moments before howling for victory, took round after round from their side and behind. Within moments, about the time it took the twenty rangers to fire two volleys, almost all of the Indians on the rocky incline had been killed or wounded.

Eli came to one knee as he reached the rangers' flank, turned and joined their witheringly accurate fire. The last few hostiles dropped or sought to run away.

"Let's close in!" Reagan shouted. "Make every shot count. Take the time to make sure of your kills."

The men behind the crest started running, chasing the Indians over the ridge.

The warriors below, having expected to be attacked by rangers from the top of the hill, now unwittingly joined the Texans in peppering the slope, aiming at the dark forms who scurried down toward them.

War Moon had crouched in what cover the mesquite afforded him. Now he stood his full height and shouted down the grade.

"Stop, Riding Wolf!" the Kiowa-Apache leader yelled. "It is your brothers! We have been tricked."

"Stop firing!" Riding Wolf screamed. "That is War Moon."

A fusillade of gunfire suddenly burst from the headquarters of the XIT Ranch, behind the decoy Indians. Its sound rolled across the ground to echo off the walls of the canyon. The coordinated fire came from a line of grim-faced cowboys who advanced steadily on their enemy. The hands of the XIT, led by Charlie Goodnight in a blue-streak of epithets, closed the gap between them and the redskins.

"Kill the red-assed bastards!" Goodnight prodded, aiming a heavy .58-90 Meynard rifle carefully and firing with remarkable accuracy.

The rangers and ranch hands had sandwiched the attacking hostiles. For the gathered throng of warriors, swollen to nearly one hundred and twenty, escape lay to the right, south of the ranch house. The north had no cover and sharply rising ground, bristling with rangers' rifles, that offered little hope of survival. Quickly Eli and the rangers near him made a dash for the southern route, making the trap snap tight.

The Indian camp fell into total disarray. War Moon joined the warriors who had been the decoys and tried to organize a breakout. Suddenly, from around the base of the hill, came a buckboard wagon, two horses near death, Jeremiah Turpin at the reins. April Turpin stood in the small space behind the driver's box, a Bible clasped in her hands, staring defiantly at the combating forces. They drove directly into the midst of the milling Indians.

"Hold your fire!" Reagan shouted.

"We can't stop now," Eli bellowed back.

"No Texan is gonna shoot a woman, scout," the captain replied.

"Thou shalt not kill!" Jeremiah bawled at the XIT headquarters and joined his wife, prepared for martyrdom.

The sudden hesitation in the white men's attack allowed the hostiles to reach their mounts. They galloped off, herding their stolen horses and booty to the south, howling in frustration. They had been rescued from annihilation, though, and their spirits rose. The power of *Maman-ti* and Red Owl had saved them.

"Get down," Oliver Loving shouted, running toward the Quakers' wagon. Jeremiah jumped back to the reins and started to move with the Indians, now racing off to the south. Loving seized the wheel horse's headstall and held the animal there. The cowboys ran up and fired at the fleeing warriors, while Jeremiah yelled appropriate curses at them garnered from his knowledge of the Old Testament.

Eli, Reagan, and his men, however, ducked and dug deep into the brush to avoid the howling braves overrunning their position. Then they stayed down until the cowhands' lead chasing the hostiles stopped. After a short pause, one ranger ran down the hill, shouting for the cowboys to stop firing because their buddies were out there. Holten raised his dirt-caked face from where he'd hidden to look over at where Captain Reagan seemed to be burrowing a hole like a demented badger.

The older man spit sand and grit from his mouth, glanced at the scout and smiled. "You all right?" he asked.

"Yeah. But I don't think he is," Holten replied through a grin as he pointed to Charlie Goodnight.

The livid look on Charlie Goodnight's face bordered on apoplexy. He came howling from his cover behind a stone well casing.

"What? Who? I could . . . you should . . . awh shee-it!"

Charlie had been prepared to wax poetic, adding a whole new dimension to the word obscenity. In his heart he knew that a tirade of angry four-letter words lined up in new and astonishing order would paint a lurid picture so colorful and lifelike that it would make the idiot dressed in black on the wagon melt from its sulfureous flames. He couldn't do it, though.

He stood there, struck mute, his entire vocabulary reduced to nothing. A moment to put Charlie Goodnight's name in the books as an artist of the language stood neutralized.

A woman was present.

"Jeremiah Turpin," Reagan yelled as he ran toward the wagon. "You are under arrest."

Goodnight sucked in his breath and hooted with glee.

He joyfully nodded his agreement with this tactic.

"On what charge, Captain?" Turpin returned coolly.

"Aiding and abetting multiple murder, for starters," Duke told him. "Obstructing officers of the law in the performance of their duty, endangering the lives of said officers and the populace here about and effecting the escape of said murderers. To that you can add accessory to murder and after the fact of murder, insurrection and riot. If that's not enough to suit you, I'll think up some more."

Goodnight clasped his hands and sighed relief. He shook an admonitory finger at Jeremiah, glanced over at the virgin-eared woman and held his tongue.

"Sinners! Blasphemers!" Jeremiah bellowed at Reagan. "Dost thee think I'm blind? Dost thee not realize that anyone could see the criminal act thy *evil* Texans plotted for those poor, mistreated Children of Nature? Why, even now they have been driven further away from the safety of their homes."

"What?" Oliver Loving croaked.

"A cold-blooded, pre-planned massacre, obviously! They will hear of this in Washington." Jeremiah sat back down. "April, stay here."

"I want to be with thee," Mrs. Turpin crooned.

"I go where danger lurks, but God and I will persevere."

"You ain't going nowhere, Turpin," Reagan countered.

"I am going to find War Moon," the Quaker replied. "Like Moses, I will lead these frightened and confused Children of Nature back to the safety of their homes in the Indian territory."

"War Moon and Red Owl ain't from the Nations, you mule-stubborn, pea-brained fanatic!" Reagan thundered. "They're Kiowa-Apaches from New Mexico. *Wild* Indians, you numbskull."

212

Jeremiah affected not to hear the ranger. "Let my people go, O Pharaoh!"

Reagan turned away, as though stunned by a powerful blow. "Oh, Jesus, now he thinks I'm the King of Egypt."

"You can't go after them, you fool," Eli growled close by the wagon seat. "War Moon and Red Owl will kill you if you try to interfere now. You've delivered them an escape here that they'll see as a victory. Their blood-lust will be up."

"Kill me?" the Indian agent scoffed. "Hast thee already forgotten last night? The Holy Spirit spoke through me and War Moon cowered back in the face of my righteousness. He is frightened, alone and needing only kindness and understanding words of guidance to end this despicable situation."

April slipped from the wagon and eased a distance away. The next instant, Jeremiah gave a brisk snap of the whip and swatted Oliver Loving across the face. With a shout and another crack of the lash, the Quaker tore out of the circle of men that had formed around him. Turpin chased after the fleeing savages, quickly putting distance between him and the whites behind.

"Let him go," Reagan shouted as some of his men ran for horses. "I can't honestly think of a more cruel thing to do to him than let him go."

Nineteen

At the owner's direction, Thacker hauled boxes of ammunition up from a cache in the floor of the ranch house. Goodnight stood nearby, mute and red-faced while Mrs. Turpin intoned quotations from the Bible, berating each man as he stepped up to restock his supplies.

"We'll ride as soon as we can," Reagan announced to the working men. "First I think we better have a war council."

Louise Van Pelton stood toward the back of the room. She still looked dreamy and drugged. Her eyes glowed with admiration as she watched while Eli checked and cleaned his weapons. Her expression was like a glutton who's had his fill but can't help drooling over dessert.

"Hey, Holten," a ranger called into the ranch house. "There's some mean-lookin' hombre out here askin' for you."

Holten absently gave a quick check for dirt in his newly cleaned revolver, loaded and holstered it and

215

walked outside.

The scout instantly recognized the man as the mysterious figure who had been with the Eastern fast-draw artist on the train in Kansas. The stranger tipped up the brim of his black ranchero's sombrero and gave Holten a relaxed, lopsided grin.

"Eli Holten," he challenged. "My name is Ike Lampbertson. You killed a friend of mine."

"That's right." Eli felt a tug at his lips. Before him stood a wealth of answers to questions that no one had ever been able to ask. The gunslinger's very presence answered a couple. He had been right to suspect the incident on the train had been no coincidence. He started walking toward the gunhawk.

"I'm calling you out, Holten," Lampbertson snarled.

"What are you talking about?" Thacker blurted.

"Fair, legal fight," Ike stated. "A duel, if you wish, with revolvers. I say 'draw,' you go for it. Whoever shoots first and hits . . ." The shootist smiled nastily. "Wins."

"That ain't fair." Wild Man stepped down next to the scout and glared at Lampbertson. "Your friend needed killing."

The Easterner pulled his coat back, clearing the way to his holster. "Draw."

Lampbertson's fellow killer had been fast. Blindingly, deadly fast. Eli figured this gun mechanic would be even better. Ike had some information the scout wanted, though, and Holten decided to gamble for it.

With a slight motion, Eli signaled Les back, then he started walking toward the deadly gunman in front of him. Brazenly he stepped up to Ike, his hand still not touching the butt of his Remington. He stuck out his jaw and practically stood nose to nose with the fast-draw practitioner.

"Took you a long time to decide to get to me, fool," Eli

said quietly. "Why'd you wait so long? Why didn't you do it at the train?"

"I'm here now," Lampbertson answered evenly.

"I think you only got your orders now. From the guy who hired you. What's his name, Ike? Is it *Tejan* or Red Owl? What do these rangers know him as?"

"You think I'd work for some red nigger?" Lampbertson scoffed.

"A red-haired, freckle-faced Indian with plenty of money from looting towns and the like."

The scout read the answer in the killer's eyes. He'd gotten it right. Holten went for his gun.

Ike moved a split second slower than he could have before the nerve-rattling conversation. Nonetheless, to those rangers and cowmen watching, the fast-draw shooter's Colt .36 Navy with the shortened barrel seemed to leap into his hand. Blinding fast, he fired.

At such close range, it seemed as though it would be impossible to miss.

The moment Eli went for his .44, he shifted his weight to the side. With his left hand he caught the muzzle of the .36 Navy's barrel as the gunslick pulled the trigger. The slug split cloth under Eli's armpit. The stinging burn of powder grains only heightened Holten's urge to survive. Before Lampbertson could re-cock his weapon, Eli had his Remington out and aimed point-blank at the shootist's gut.

Holten fired.

Ike shivered as though confronted with a profound and frightening mystery. His back bulged, then erupted with bloody flesh and fragments of vertebrae that splashed all over the dusty ground behind him.

Ike Lampbertson uttered a soft sigh and his eyes rolled up to show the whites. He sagged at the knees and collapsed dead to the dusty ocher soil, his feet and legs jerking spasmodically.

Mrs. Turpin screamed in horror at the carnage. Louise gasped.

Then she sucked air in and began to pant rapidly. In the next moment, as a hand darted to her breasts and dwelled on the tip of one, Louise started walking toward Holten.

"Oh, Eli," she breathed out in a high moan. The excitement . . . all that blood an' killing and fighting an' sweaty male bodies . . . grunting and straining. *Oh, lord, Eli, I want you . . . now!"*

She threw herself at Holten, like some wild beast with claws and venom. Around him, the rangers and cowmen chuckled knowingly, enjoying the scout's sudden embarrassment. Eli grabbed the nape of her neck, drew her back, then unceremoniously dumped her in a water trough. He plunged a boot in, pushed down on her stomach and kept her bottom pinned to the floor of the rough plank container.

"Mr. Goodnight," Eli called out. The owner of the XIT stepped carefully toward him. "You got a room where you can keep a person locked up tight?"

"The Injuns emptied out the tack room. It ain't got windows and the door can be barred from the outside."

"Get a chamber pot in there, some blankets and then throw this girl in . . . and lock the door tight."

Goodnight leaned toward the scout and whispered through a snicker. "Sounds fuckin' cruel, Mister."

"You want your men fit to fight? Then get ready to lock this one up, or she'll screw 'em cross-eyed. Get one of your *female* servants to do it and to go feed her," Holten added.

Goodnight frowned skeptically at Holten, then brightened. "Or is it cruel fuckin'?" he offered. The rancher shot a quick glance at the dead body of the gunslinger and dismissed him. He turned to Quaid and whispered orders to fulfill Eli's requests.

"And lock up that old harridan, too," he concluded, pointing at April Turpin. Then, like the rest of the party, he looked up sharply.

From the west the sound of charging horses began to mount.

"Riders coming down the canyon trail!" a lookout yelled from the roof. "Looks like Lieutenant Wilderspin."

The rangers and XIT ranch hands started shouting and whooping rebel yells as they went to greet the arriving contingent. Eli stood back with a sodden and defused Louise.

Twenty fast riders charged around a bend and lined out to the corral, falling from their horses, hugging the men who greeted them with colorful epithets and peels of hearty laughter. Wilderspin slid from his mount and marched quickly to Captain Reagan.

"Duke," he said with a casual, offhand salute. "What are you doing here?"

"This is the way those redskins in the territory brought us," Reagan said, returning the salute. "How are you?"

"Tired, hungry, and disgusted. We were out on another wild goose chase," Wilderspin sighed. He looked up to see Tom Meyers, his sombrero drooping low over his eyes. "Old Tom, he got us back here. We'd still be out chasing shadows if it weren't for Meyers." The lieutenant shouted out. "Hey, Tom! Get on over here."

Eli saw the volunteer scout's face peer out from under his Mexican hat. The young redhead's exhaustion looked etched to the bone.

"Rode all night to tell us Goodnight was being bushwhacked," Wilderspin concluded. Meyers slid from his saddle and stepped forward to report to Captain Reagan.

A quick round of introductions followed. Reagan told

Wilderspin and Meyers about Eli Holten, Eli met the lieutenant and Tom. He shook Wilderspin's hand heartily, then turned his outstretched palm to shake Tom's. Meyers forced a tired smile to his face and clasped the army scout's hand. Eli took note of the strength of the young man despite his apparent exhaustion and also noticed that the little finger on Tom's left hand lacked its first joint.

Jeremiah Turpin egged his dying mounts forward. The animals took each step as though it would be their last. Each one could have been, only the Quaker and his religious zeal willed them on, closer to his goal.

It had been three hours since he left the mass-murdering Texans behind him, he considered, in his quest to seek out the lost lambs who lay somewhere ahead. He could only hope that they had not suffered too many losses. His horses began to blow and snort and totter drunkenly against the wagon tongue. The Indian agent finally dismounted at this turn of events and walked the two suffering animals forward, letting them catch their breath. As he stumbled on he heard something ahead.

Turpin's heart leaped with joy. He began to trot the two doomed, gasping beasts. They protested and he let them stop. Jeremiah crawled up on the driver's seat. From his vantage point he peered into the distance.

Out ahead, in a sandy-bottomed depression, a group of red men danced and howled.

With the last sparks of life, Jeremiah's team hauled him into the camp of War Moon and the followers of Red Owl. The warriors stopped their gyrations and stared openmouthed.

"Red Owl predicted this to me," Riding Wolf muttered from the bed of Leroy Barker's wagon, a jug of whiskey in his hands. "He said we would be victorious, but not like we expected to be."

"Then it came to pass!" War Moon shouted, his speech slurred by the amount of liquor he had consumed. The war chief saw the black-clad Quaker standing in front of his wagon and he cried out a war whoop of greeting.

"You have come to help us celebrate our victory, White Peace Pipe!" War Moon cried as he stumbled up to Turpin. "You must drink the burning water with us and dance to the death of the white men."

Like an ice-covered statue, Jeremiah stood, eyes blazing righteous wrath.

"Whiskey!" he intoned coldly and angrily, horrified to find War Moon in the company of Leroy Barker, a man he'd warned him once to avoid. "Demon Rum! A disease that eats at the moral fiber of the Children of Nature. An abomination."

War Moon stood unsteadily before the pontificating Indian agent, speechless and caught off guard.

"A tool of the devil! I call upon you, War Moon, to cast down the drink of Satan . . . Little Yellow Bush!" he ended in a flash of misguided inspiration.

War Moon glanced down at the tight throat of the crockery jug and, for a moment, he actually saw a resemblance between it and the white demon he had so cunningly rid himself of. The thought made his stomach boil. Before he could speak, or even cast aside the offending substance as he had been bidden, Turpin continued his tirade.

"I appeal to your peaceful nature. Lay down your tools of violence and return to your wives and children, to a peaceful way that will give you dignity, humility, and God. Keep to your houses and grow your food in the land you love so much."

War Moon looked up angrily at the mention of digging in the dirt like some snake or prairie dog. The warrior straightened as best his drunken state would allow and answered tersely.

"Do you or the White Grandfather in Washington give gifts to the peaceful tribes up north, who dig in the dirt and do not raid? No! Only the stinking meat and flour and old clothes cast off by your fellow whites. You also give them sicknesses our people have never known before." He stopped a moment and struck his chest with a balled fist. "You and your Lodge of Brothers—your Society of Friends—and the White Grandfather give War Moon, *Satank* and other war chiefs many gifts *after* we raid. You give us presents and food for signing peace treaties. Our warriors get steel hatchets and new blankets. You never ask the dirt-digging people to come and talk peace."

"If you sign a treaty of peace, are you not bound by your word to keep the peace?"

"If we kept the treaties, you would not want us to sign any more and then you wouldn't give us gifts," War Moon snapped in simple logic. "The Mexicans pay ransoms for the children we steal and you feed our old people and babies when we are out raiding. I will raid and make war for the rest of my life, as I was meant to, as I was born to."

Jeremiah stood there gaping for a moment at the brain-numbing logic. As a Quaker he felt rattled to his very soul. Slowly his righteous wrath mounted and he started raising his voice.

"Those who live by the sword, shall die by the sword!" he cried. The warriors who understood the Kiowa language nodded and commented at the wisdom of these words.

"What more can a warrior ask for than to die by that for which he lived?" Riding Wolf observed with a confirming nod.

The Indian agent's anger erupted. His face turned livid and his voice cracked as he abandoned his beloved "Peace-At-Any-Price" rhetoric and slipped into some

Baptist fire-and-brimstone exhortations.

"The fire of Hell will consume your flesh!" Turpin cried, pointing an accusing finger at War Moon.

"The fire you speak of or the scavengers of the plains," War Moon allowed agreeably. "It is all the same."

"The sins of the fathers shall be visited upon the sons unto the seventh generation!" Turpin thundered.

War Moon grew tired of the discussion. Riding Wolf laughed and pointed with his chin at Jeremiah.

"He speaks too much and listens too little. If the white man has not come to celebrate our victory, then perhaps he should leave."

"Yes," War Moon agreed as he put down the liquor. He picked up his Winchester and chambered a round. "I think that would be good."

The .44-40 slug smacked into the Quaker's breastbone. It lifted Jeremiah Turpin off the ground and threw him into his two dying horses. His back opened and spewed blood out over them even before he hit. The two animals buckled under Turpin's dead weight and fell in a heap with him.

Eli, along with Les Thacker, Duke Reagan, Tom Meyers, Charlie Goodnight, Lieutenant Wilderspin, and Oliver Loving all sat in the empty kitchen of the ranch house and had a council of war. The assessment of their condition and supplies left none of them happy, though they remained firm on one point.

"We should fucking well get right after those heathen sonsofbitches," Goodnight growled. "We could climb their asses before the day is through and butcher them on the run. With all my outriders coming in, and with Wilderspin's contingent of rangers, plus the rest gettin' here from south of Menardville, we can take those ball-busting peckerheads right now. If we wait much longer, it's gonna be tough to locate them. They might break up and we'll never catch them."

"I disagree," Holten asserted with a sharp voice. "Their blood is up, they're not going to scatter until they've made a lot more *coups*. I want to go after them as bad as you, but we should hold off a day. Wilderspin's men nearly killed themselves and their horses getting here. We all need a little food and sleep. Me and Meyers can keep War Moon and his men in sight. I think we've got these renegades in a bear trap. It's only a matter of hitting them when we're in the best shape."

The others around the table glanced up at the army scout with looks of confusion and irritation and, on Goodnight's face, disgust.

"I find myself torn here," Reagan stated. "We've never run down this large a number of warriors since back before the War Between the States. Must be a hundred of them. I don't think we can chase them to death. We need a military approach. Still, my first inclination is to start after them, to be able to get into position, seize the opportunity when we can to attack."

"Captain Reagan," Holten insisted coldly. "I've traveled a damned long way because General Corrington said you could use me to help understand the Indians of the plains. Now I hope you'll think enough of the general to let me help and take my advice."

"Now, see here, scout," Wilderspin started as he rose from his seat. Reagan touched his lieutenant's arm without pulling his eyes off the suddenly pushy Holten. Wilderspin slowly returned to his seat as the captain and the scout stared into each other's eyes. After a long pause, Duke nodded sagely, calculatingly.

"All right, scout," the captain relented. "We'll go your way."

Charlie Goodnight launched into a blue streak of picturesque phrases.

Twenty

Meyers studied Holten out of the corner of his eye as the volunteer scout checked the supplies strapped behind his saddle.

"You don't like what I have in mind, Meyers?" Eli asked innocently.

"N-no," Meyers stammered. "I mean, yes. I . . . what I'm tryin' to say is I agree with gettin' out there, keepin' War Moon in sight. I just don't like the way you told Captain Reagan about it."

"I got a little sharp," Holten admitted. "The trail is getting to me and I'm a long way from home. Maybe I'm getting old. I really think this is the better plan."

"I agree." Tom rocked his head. "I got a pretty good idea where those red niggers'll be settling in for the night."

"Good," Eli answered, digging at the bottom of his saddlebags. "Let's go."

Meyers spun into the saddle. Holten, however, pulled an envelope from a saddlebag. "Damn," the scout cursed.

"What?" Tom asked.

The army scout waved the envelope. "A letter from General Corrington to Captain Reagan. I forgot all about it. I'll rush it in real quick."

"Give it to him later," Meyers protested.

"There may not be a later," Holten retorted. He ran into the XIT ranch house.

Meyers waited patiently for a few minutes, then became suspicious. He slipped from his horse and started walking toward the entrance of the ranch headquarters. Before he reached the door, Holten came rushing out.

"Let's go," Eli suggested as he trotted past Meyers.

"What took you so damned long?"

"Old men and old friends make for long wind," Eli called back. "It took longer than I thought."

Holten jumped into his saddle and Meyers followed.

"How long you figure it'll take us to catch up with them?" Holten asked as they rode out of the compound.

"If they're where I think they are, maybe a couple of hours."

Holten looked to the west. "The sun should be setting about then."

The two experienced trackers followed the clear trail of both the many Indian ponies and a single imprint of wagon wheels. The sinuous path of the Red River through Palo Duro Canyon took them even further south, tending eastward a bit. The sun inched down their backs as shadows grew.

"The Injuns used to worship their gods down in this canyon," Meyers observed. "There's all sorts of caves up along the walls. Paintings in them and animals carved in stone. Some of them even I don't believe are real. Like oversized snakes with legs."

"Let's hope War Moon didn't pick one of them to hold up in. That could give us some nasty surprises."

"That's for sure." Meyers remained silent a moment,

226

then spoke again. "What about that crazy preacher or whatever the cap'n mentioned?"

"If we find Turpin alive," Eli stated, "it'll be because his horses died. He's got some idea that he's Moses or something, leadin' the Children of Israel out of the wilderness."

Meyers snorted. "Some prophet *he* makes. I hate a man who mistreats his horse," Tom went on. "Tells you something about how he treats people."

Holten smiled and nodded knowingly.

After two hours of riding, Tom took Eli to some high ground and, from that vantage point, the two white men could see the war party below on the floor of the canyon. More Indian adherents had joined the followers of Red Owl. The camp had swollen to one hundred and fifty.

"I've never heard of that many warriors in one place since the Little Big Horn," Eli gasped.

"With that many braves, Red Owl could wipe the Panhandle clean of white men," Tom answered, a note of awe in his voice.

"Let's get closer," Holten suggested as he pulled his boots off and replaced them with his moccasins.

The two scouts moved silently, easing through the brush and cover until they sat nearly next to the camp. From a low, boulder-strewn ridge, they observed the activity below.

The wild celebration, fueled by the ever present Leroy Barker and his jugs of cheap whiskey, bordered on madness. For a group of warriors only recently driven from their goal, Holten calculated, they seemed very assured indeed. He used silent hand signals to indicate they should move to another vantage point.

Holten led the way, quietly stepping through the sage and mesquite, noting that Barker's wagon team had been unhitched and that a fire blazed high and hot in the middle of the ring of dancing braves. The warriors looked settled for the night and totally unconcerned for their safety.

Holten grimaced at Turpin's wagon and the Quaker's desecrated body. He had been stripped and mutilated, his testicles hacked off and poked into his mouth, eyes gouged out and eviscerated, his empty body strapped to a wagon wheel.

Tom and Eli stayed most of the night at the edge of the camp. All the time, Holten studied the terrain and counted heads. The two men crouched for what seemed to Meyers a fruitlessly long time, then the army scout motioned them away. He led the redheaded scout a good three hundred yards, came to a wash and crawled down into it.

"Not safe to be down in a gully in spring," Tom warned.

"I don't want our prey to overhear us," Holten answered.

A full moon lit the night and the scout could see Meyers's face clearly. "If we rush back and tell the ranger's they've settled down this close, Reagan can have his men in position by sunup."

"What about them resting up?" the volunteer scout asked with a show of concern for the rangers, though Holten read the truth in the younger man's eyes.

"They don't need to rest to lay in the brush and wait for morning," Eli offered. "Besides, those warriors are dancing a war dance. I'll lay odds they plan to turn around and hit some new target."

"No, they'll stay after the rangers until they're eliminated," Tom insisted. "They got them all in one place now, like Red Owl wanted." His mouth snapped shut and Tom Meyers knew the truth, too.

Holten went for his gun, yet knew he couldn't use it without alerting the Indian camp. His hesitation let the redhead pull his J. H. Dance .44 and aim it point-blank.

228

"How long have you known?"

"Wasn't sure until just now," Holten answered as he raised his hands, "Red Owl. Or do you prefer *Tejan*?"

"How the hell did you put all *that* together?" Meyers hissed.

"Red Owl and the owl prophet, old *Maman-ti*? His adopted son and best student, *Tejan*, a captured white boy with red hair and freckles? Somebody had to be getting firsthand information from the rangers to outsmart a man like Reagan.

"Somebody knew he'd gone into the territory, and somebody knew to draw off another big hunk of the rangers to the west. Then you ride in, bright red hair and all, not looking too happy to see all those rangers in one place and still alive. When did you chop off your little finger, *Tejan*? When you went dream walking or to mourn *Maman-ti*'s death?"

The white Kiowa-Apache, member of the Buffalo Medicine Lodge, started to answer. Then sensed, rather than heard, something in the brush above him. His eyes shot back to Holten.

"You knew all along!" He nearly cursed this accusation out. "You went back to tell Reagan to follow us. The rangers are moving into position now."

"For their favorite attack," Holten acknowledged. Eli fought an urge to leer at the youth. "Even those blue cavalry pants gave me a hint. Lieutenant Baldwin gave you a uniform after he captured you, thinking you'd like to dump your Indian clothes."

"Don't you see, Tall Bear?" *Tejan* pleaded. "I can exterminate the white men out here and soon we'll wipe them out everywhere. We'll free your home and your people in the Black Hills in time and the buffalo will spread black over the plains."

"All you're going to do is get your people destroyed," Holten stated flatly.

229

"No. Can't you see, Tall Bear? You are one of us. I was only five when I was taken by the Kiowa. It was fun being an Indian. I got to swim and ride horses and wrestle with the other boys. It . . . *it felt good*! Like I belonged for the first time. *Maman-ti* adopted me. He taught me the secrets of the medicine language and how to work his magic. Even our cousins, the Comanche, came to respect me. Before I was twelve, I made a vow. I . . . I've never had a woman. It is part of my personal medicine to refrain from satisfying my lusts. I have only my hand to ease my physical demands. But it has been worth it! It must have been much like that for you. Now you can be free of the curse of the white man and his civilization once and for all. Join us! You are one of the People, just as I am."

"I feel sorry for you, *Tejan*. You see, I am not at all like you. I was past twelve when the Oglala found me. I grew up the son of a civil chief in a peaceful village. I have no hate for the white man . . . and none for my red brothers. I only do what I must do. Give me the gun. Surrender to me and I'll do what I can to see you can live with your chosen people for the rest of your life, that you won't be hanged."

"Hanged!" the word came out strangled, as though Red Owl already had the rope tightening around his neck. In the next instant, the young medicine man jerked his weapon up to Holten's face. The shot would kill Tall Bear and warn his people all in one stroke.

Eli's motion blurred in the pale light of the moon. He slammed his hand down between the hammer and the back plate. Eli grimaced as the sharp firing pin lodged in the web between thumb and finger instead of the primer of a cartridge. The pain distracted him as he pulled his own weapon free of its holster.

Red Owl kicked savagely at Eli. His booted foot knocked the Remington away and into the sand. The Dance .44 fell off Holten's bleeding hand.

230

Tejan pulled his knife and stabbed viciously at Holten's abdomen. The blade flashed a blue streak of moonlight as it sped toward its target.

Holten parried the thrust with his injured hand, then pulled his own knife and slashed at Red Owl's chest. He cut half an inch deep into the younger warrior's flesh, only to be kicked in the gut. He fell down and *Tejan* ran for the gully's wall. His clawed fingers dug at the crumbling sand as he scampered up it.

Holten brought his bowie stabbing overhand, going for *Tejan*'s kidneys. The white Indian turned and kicked the knife away. Eli grabbed *Tejan*'s leg and the two men fell back into the wash.

As they fought, neither white warrior noticed the false dawn flash on the horizon and begin to fade into the blackness before real sunrise. In utter concentration they battled in silence. Red Owl rolled on top and brought his knife up for a quick thrust into Holten's throat. Eli grabbed the medicine man's wrist and, for a moment, the blade hovered inches from the scout, then plunged down as Holten shoved himself to one side. The knife sank into the soft sand.

Holten pulled up and cracked a fist into *Tejan*'s jaw. Red hair flung outward as *Tejan*'s head snapped back. In the moment's respite, Holten flung himself aside to find his bowie.

Red Owl twisted in the opposite direction and slid over something in the sand that felt cold and smooth. With a jerk, the warrior scooped up his J. H. Dance revolver, grinned insanely at Holten as the scout reeled to his feet, then pulled the hammer back and fired.

The Dance's barrel had packed with sand when Holten stumbled on it. When Tom Meyers had rolled over the weapon it had only compounded the fault.

The Confederate-made J. H. Dance and Company revolver exploded in the white Kiowa-Apache's face. The flash reflected off the white sand and lit the hate-twisted, surprised face of the warrior. Holten rushed Red Owl with his retrieved bowie knife and split the prophet's flesh at the sternum.

With a powerful wrench, he twisted the blade and pulled it free. Rich dark blood pumped rhythmically from Tom Meyers.

The warriors in camp looked toward the source of the sound. The rangers and cowhands mistook it for their signal.

A swarm of lead came cracking out of the brush and rocks to the north and east. It launched splinters of wood in all directions from Barker's wagon. Slugs blew ugly holes in the warriors who still stood after celebrating and dancing all night. They had been lost in their ritual preparations for more war and now looked dully up as the world around them angrily barked death.

Leroy Barker raced away from his disintegrating wagon and supplies of whiskey, guns, and ammunition. He scurried for a horse. Most of the animals already sported bloody wounds as the lead aimed at warriors flew past the targets and hit the wall of horseflesh at the western corner of the camp. Barker found a pony still in one piece. He struggled to crawl on as the herd, terrified, began to hobble further away.

A shot cracked close to his head and the white trader slid off and under the sharp feet of the nervously prancing animals. Hoof after hoof, hardly lifted off the dirt, ground into the screaming white man as he tried in vain to crawl out from under the milling beasts. His shrieks of agony went unheard in the fury of battle.

The warriors in camp took up their weapons and started returning fire. They crawled behind the prone corpses of their ponies and sheltered around Barker's wagon. The rangers took their time, studying their targets, sighting well, then shooting with deadly accuracy. They chambered new rounds and chose the next unfortunate.

The soil bounced with the onslaught of lead that came from a brutal, inverted V that outflanked the gathered braves. The sun crested the horizon, blinding the camp defenders and aiding the white attackers. For a solid hour, they pressed their deadly assault.

Holten crawled out of the gully, crouched and ran to the now familiar figures of Captain Reagan and Les Thacker. He hunkered down and touched the ranger officer lightly on one shoulder.

"Guess you were right, Eli," Reagan sighed.

"I'm sorry, Captain," Holten answered as he raised the Winchester he had been given to take aim. "Tom Meyers was Red Owl."

"Damn," Thacker cursed. He also sighted in and fired at the darting figures of red men in the camp. "I thought he was a Texan."

"He might have been, at one time," Eli offered awkwardly. "He told me a story before he died. From it, I'd gather his life hadn't been entirely a good one before the Kiowa took him in and old *Maman-ti* adopted him. He was a little tad and the Indian thing . . . just sort of got to him."

"How'd he take up with the Kiowa-Apaches?"

"He didn't say. My guess is that came about after *Maman-ti* got shipped off to Florida. That broke Kiowa power and they went into the Nations. Most of the Comanches, too. That wouldn't be good enough for a boy who had grown half his life as a special sort of person. Whatever the case, he made a good hostile."

"For certain sure," Thacker agreed. "But all that happened only a little over a year ago. He can't be, uh, couldn't have been over nineteen or so."

"I've seen a Sioux boy of eleven kill three men, Crows attacking the village I grew up in. If a boy has the warrior

233

spirit, it doesn't matter his age or the color of his skin."

Within ten minutes, resistance from inside the camp began to fade. Braves tried to escape, only to be picked off by the sharpshooting rangers and Texas cowhands. Slowly silence, except for the groans of the wounded, filled Palo Duro Canyon.

Little Louise Van Pelton shivered with fear, her blue eyes huge with trepidation. She looked up anxiously at Eli Holten.

"Just be polite, remember your manners and do like I tell you to, understand?"

The girl nodded with silver tears forming in her eyes. Eli draped a hand over her shoulder to comfort her then led her into the Good Times Saloon on Murdock in Wichita.

Della Caldwell glanced toward the swinging gates of her establishment, then did a double take. Mixed emotions rippled across her face.

Eli Holten could bring a gush of pleasure to any woman who'd been with him, except maybe when he led a child. The madam nonetheless smiled and started prancing toward her favorite dream.

"Why, Eli, you've come back," she cooed.

"Howdy, Della," Holten greeted, then motioned at the young girl at his side. "I'd like you to meet a friend of mine."

Louise curtsied. "How do you do, Miss Caldwell. I'm Louise Van Pelton."

"Isn't she polite?" Holten enthused.

"Isn't she," Della agreed icily. She forced a smile at Louise. "Sweetheart, would you like a sarsaparilla?"

The girl's eyes lit up. She glanced at Holten for reassurance, then nodded vigorously.

"Well, then, you go over to the bar and tell Mike I said

234

you could have one. Just say Della sent you."

Louise scampered off and immediately Della stepped coldly up to Eli. "Holten, you're sick. Bringing a child like that into a place like this. Why, I never dreamed your tastes ran to . . . to something that bizarre."

"Della, she's not all that young, she's got no home, she's a nice girl and—"

"You want *me* to take her in *here*?" the soiled dove hissed. "I'm a business woman, for the love of Pete."

"Della," Holten organized his rehearsed speech again. "Little Louise has long ago lost her innocence. She has an urge that can't be fought, she never tires and she could make you *a lot of money*."

Only a few hours later, with a new batch of cowboys in from the trail, most of them hardly older than Louise, Della received a practical demonstration of the girl's "urge."

Della watched through a small peephole the room into which Louise had been directed to take her guests. The girl arrived with three boys, one not more than twelve. Deftly she stripped them of everything but their hats, which they held onto tenaciously. With squeals and youthful zest, she undressed herself and took turns with each cowhand, giggling and chattering so disarmingly that even the youngest, most nervous boy soon found himself with an aching erection. Eagerly he climbed between her legs and, with her guiding, stabbed at her open portal.

With a cry of delight he began rutting on her bare chest like a wild boar, his reddened penis tinglingly at home in a warm, juicy purse. After far too short a time he whimpered with delight, shuddered and withdrew his still dripping shaft.

Louise turned on her side and quickly induced the

other youngsters to take her front and rear at the same time. Hesitant at first, they soon entered the game with eagerness and energy that brought grunts of happiness from little Louise. Her most recent partner knelt on the bed and watched avidly, idly stroking himself to new fullness, the dark red tip of his throbbing organ popping in and out of his rapidly moving foreskin.

"My God, she's versatile," Della gasped, feeling herself grow warm from the exhibition she witnessed. "You sure you weren't her teacher, Holten?" she asked shrewdly.

"Swear it, Della."

Another demonstration, with more young guests, lasted most of the night. After three hours, Della started licking her lips and shifting her legs as she watched, mesmerized in her bent-over stance by the show on the other side of the wall.

"At this rate, she's doing the work of three girls," the madam calculated aloud when Louise's whispered instructions put one boy back in his clothes to go in search of his saddle. Eli stepped behind Della, reached around and started molding her breasts.

"Isn't she all I said she'd be?" Holten muttered as he rubbed his crotch against the soiled dove's extended rear.

"She's still a little crude . . . and too damned young," Della noted critically. "And she needs a lot more control She's enjoying it too much. But it's nothing a few years won't solve."

"Anywhere else she's gonna be treated as an outcast, Della," Holten pressed, pulling the madam's skirt up until her red silk bloomers popped out, stretched by her shapely firm rump. With a solid tug, Holten yanked the panties down. They fell to Della's ankles and she absently stepped out of them.

Holten opened his fly and worked his swollen, blood engorged member free. He started sliding its silky surface between the woman's legs. "Here I know she'll be treated with a certain respect, have a home and good food. And let's face it, she'll never get married on you. No man all by himself would be enough for her."

"Voice of experience?" Della taunted through a throaty chuckle. Her body trembled all over and she longed for the fullness of this mighty lover while she observed further exploits of her newest inmate in the other room. She reached down between her legs, grabbed Holten's manhood and guided it to the petals of her experienced flower. The two hesitated, then Holten eased his fleshy lance into the inviting wet cavern that sucked and undulated with his presence. Holten loosened Della's top, then pulled her breasts free. The madam never took her eye off the peephole.

Louise lay atop one young cowboy, his red, glowing phallus completely encased in her hard-working mouth, her lips nuzzling the sparse thatch of newly acquired pubic hair at its thick base. She flung her legs wide, and from the depths of their sweaty passion, the youngster's ardent lapping at her dripping cleft could be clearly heard by Della Caldwell beyond the wall.

"Then you'll take her in?" Holten asked as he grabbed the woman's hips and dug his loving weapon to the dome of her womb.

"Oh, yes, Holten," Della gasped, staring wide-eyed into the spy hole to the next room. "Only don't stop. I . . . I might take some more convincin'."

The grunting couple in Louise's room worked to a squealing crescendo in time with the efforts of the scout and Della Caldwell. Della's mouth opened wide as she fought for air, yet she didn't look away from the hole until she reached her limit and started bucking like a wild horse needing to be broken.

"Hurry up, Larry, it's my turn again," a squeaky young voice complained from inside the love nest. "I'm tired of whackin' off while you have all the fun."

"Wait until the saddle gets here, boys," Louise cooed. "Then you'll learn some real fun."

"Harder, Holten, harder!" Della cried.

Before he let himself get lost in the soft sweet nectar of his lover, Holten assured himself he'd done the best he could by Louise, then pondered whether to head back to Dakota Territory or wander around this part of the world for a while. After all, Louise *was* growing up.

THE CONTINUING SHELTER SERIES
by Paul Ledd

THE HOTTEST SERIES IN THE WEST CONTINUES!
by Jory Sherman